PROPHECY

THE HUNTSMAN CLAN BOOK FOUR

ROSE ALEXANDER

Editing: Muddy Waters Editing

Cover: Black Glitter Press

✿ Created with Vellum

PROPHECY

One queen will unite the thrones when darkness falls. She will have five kings, class unseen. The strongest will bow, though many will compete, she will triumph as the only queen.

CHAPTER ONE

Six months ago, I was standing in front of my family, waiting to shift into a bear. But that's not what happened, and my life became turned upside down. I watch the man and woman that are my birth mother and father speaking quietly to each other as I try to process the mess that my life ended up becoming. The only bright light in it is that I found the five men that I get to call my mates. I found a brother and sister that love me as if I'm blood to them. And, I found a woman that turned out meaning more to me than I could have imagined.

Unfortunately for me, I just said my last goodbye to her. The pain inside of me is more than I can take some moments, but I've held it together. Now I'm staring at the woman that left me when I was a baby and the man I thought was just a feral cat who is apparently my father.

How did I get here? How did we get here? I can't help but wonder how different these last six months would have been had she just told me who she was... had she not hid her identity as one of my great grandmother's body guards. And my great grandmother... did she know? She knew how I struggled with finding out who I was and why my mother had left me. How could she have hidden this from me?

Now I won't get the opportunity to ask her, and I can't be mad at a woman that gave me a second family. But as bizarre as all of this seems in the sudden expanse of time, the ties within in me pull me to the two people standing in front of me trying to sort out, much like me, what the fuck happened all those years ago. The bond I share as their daughter calls to me, and I can feel Kylah trying to reach out to their cats… but it's silent.

Amid the chaos of them speaking and bickering back and forth, my hearing has suddenly left me and everything seems so quiet, only the beating of my own heart echoes in my ears.

I feel the hand that reaches out and takes hold of my own before I see it. "Amelia," Demetria cries out, wrapping me in her arms. "I've wanted to do this so many times."

I pat the strange woman on the back, still in too much shock to do much else.

"This is all too much. I think you both have a lot of explaining to do," I say as I pull back.

"Yes, we both do," Nathanial says, eyeing Demetria with a look of pain and longing.

"Where do we start?" Demetria asks him.

"Lia would probably appreciate from the beginning," he replies.

She nods her head, sitting quietly for a moment. I sit on the edge of my seat waiting for her to speak.

"We were young when we met at the academy," Demetria explains. "Panther princesses were already going missing. I had already decided I would never take a mate. I didn't want to risk having a child and putting them in danger."

"That obviously worked out for you," Kenton says, a snide look on his face. I need to find out what's going on with him when this is over.

"Obviously the best laid plans of mice and men and all of that. Anyways, I met Nathanial our first year at Nightfall. My cat was insistent we needed to be with him but I wasn't having any of it," she says.

"She shot down my advances for nearly six months," Nathanial chimes in.

"He wore me down eventually, but I made him promise to keep our bond a secret. We couldn't risk anyone knowing with the state of things. Queen Rani had taken the throne four years previous, and it was troubling times. The panther princesses... my sister included, start turning up missing, then dead. What was once a large royal family was whittled down to just my grandmother and me. We now know the connection, but back then..." Her eyes gloss over as if she's reliving a memory.

Nathanial clears his throat. "We started dating while at the academy, keeping our relationship a secret. We managed to spend a lot of time together still." He smiles at Demetria. "Then one day Demetria vanished without a trace."

"I found out I was pregnant and couldn't bear the thought of something happening to my baby." She squeezes my hand tightly in her own. "I may have thought that I didn't want kids when I met your father, but the moment I found out I was pregnant with you... all of that became irrelevant. There was nothing I wouldn't have done to protect you. But I knew, you were safer somewhere far from all of this, far from the politics of it all... a lot of good this had done for my own sister or myself." She shook her head, releasing her grip slightly. "I ran, moving from town to town, never staying in the same place for more than a week until I went into labor. You were born healthy and perfect. I knew then I would do anything to protect you, even if that meant leaving you for someone else to raise." Her eyes well with unshed tears and I feel my own burning my eyes. "Dropping you off at the orphanage was the hardest thing I've ever done. I told them you were a bear shifter to buy you sixteen years. I knew eventually you would be found, but at the time I had hoped I could resolve all of this before that happened."

"Obviously you didn't," I chime in, pulling my hand from hers and backing away, hating the sound of sadness in my own voice.

"Your great grandmother found me that same night. Turns out she had been tracking me the entire time I was running. I told her everything and she agreed you were safer being raised as a bear, and then we came up with a plan to take down whoever was killing the panthers. But first I had to stay hidden in plain sight," she says.

"How did you manage that?" Dom asks, leaning forward as he listens.

"My mother knew a witch from this secret island coven. Myrna came up with a potion that would make anyone with any bonds with me feel as if I had died. I held onto it, not wanting to put Nathanial through that pain. She also gave me the potion that allows me to appear as AJ," she answers. "I think they need to hear your story before I continue, Nathanial."

"Fair enough," he replies. "After Demetria left, I was heartbroken. I threw myself into the enforcers and made a name for myself. While in training, I met Celene. She was my rock, my best friend, but her very existence was in jeopardy. Celene was a lesbian, and that wasn't accepted in our clan, at all. At the time, it was a crime punishable by death."

"That's awful," I gasp.

"It is, little one. That's something no one should have a say in." He gives me a sad smile. "We came up with a plan to keep her safe. I married her straight away, so everyone assumed she was my bonded. No one bothered testing us and we moved overseas for my work immediately after."

"So you went feral when she was killed," Vance says.

"You're skipping ahead a little bit, but yes and no. We were on a mission to track down a supposed panther sighting; in the back of my mind, I was hoping it was Demetria. I was distracted and didn't see them until it was too late..." he trails off, covering his face with his hands.

"I was following Nathanial throughout this time period. Try as I might, I couldn't bring myself to stay away from him. They were walking down a trail through a forest where humans were hunting. One of the humans saw movement and shot, but it was Celene in her human form that was hit. She was killed immediately, and I saw my chance. I took the potion Myrna gave me, so Nathanial would appear to be mourning his lost bond with Celene, and would no longer think I was out there somewhere," Demetria explains.

"It destroyed me. My best friend and my mate were killed at the same time and I couldn't cope. I shifted and let my lion take over. My very humanity receded after a time, and I lived at the academy ever since," he says.

"How did you get back to the academy as a lion?" I ask.

"My brother, Heathcliff, came looking for me." His gaze wanders over to Sir, standing in the corner of the room. His face was stoic as usual, but I could see the interest in his eyes as Demetria and Nathaniel finally told their story after all these years of hiding it. "I had enough of my humanity to go with him willingly, but I refused to shift," he explains. "It wasn't until Amelia showed up, looking just like my lost Demetria, that my humanity began to resurface, little by little."

I always felt like he was watching me at the academy. It all makes sense now. He saw his dead mate in me, and his lion felt our bond, even if he couldn't. Kylah missed it too.

"After I took the potion to make everyone believe I was dead, I became AJ and worked in the castle with my grandmother, trying to take down Queen Rani. I'm sorry we failed you, Lia. I tried so hard to end this before it could affect you," she says, tears running down her face.

"This is all just too much," I say, standing up and bolting out of the room.

"Lia, wait!" Spence calls after me.

I turn at the door as he's running at me to catch up.

"Why should I? She knew who I was to her this whole time, and she didn't care enough to say something. Her own grandmother was killed, and she still didn't say anything!" I scream, tears streaming down my cheeks. "I can't do this. Everything is secrets and lies."

"That might be true, but this is your opportunity to... I don't know. But you can't tell me you haven't been wondering who your birth parents were and now they are here..." he struggles, rubbing the back of his neck.

"I can't right now. This is literally too much," I say then bolt away.

CHAPTER TWO

I couldn't bring myself to go back into that room. It had all been just too much. Saying my final good-byes to my great grandmother, finding out my father is the feral lion that had stalked me at the academy, and then my mother shows up as a magical transgendered bodyguard, it is all too much. I feel so sad, angry, and confused...all of these emotions warring inside of me that I couldn't hold a normal conversation if I wanted to, which I don't at the time. I spend the rest of the afternoon, lying in bed. All five of my guys stay near me, giving me my space but close enough in case I need them. I don't know what I would do without them. Just being near them brings me a level of comfort I didn't know was possible.

After waking up this morning, I feel better. A little less confused and a little more determined. I ask that AJ, or my mother, my dad, and Sir all come back so that we can finish the conversation from yesterday.

Now I'm waiting in my grandmother's study until the others arrive. The guys are still all gathered around me, each of them having barely left my side unless it was to take a shower or find us food.

The study door opens and in walks my father and Sir, both also looking a bit more relaxed today than yesterday. Moments later we are joined by AJ. He closes the door behind him before pulling a vial from his pocket and downing it. His body contorts and shifts until Demetria stands before us.

"How many of those vials do you have?" Vance asks with a bit of awe in his voice.

"Enough to get me through for now," she replies.

She moves towards me as if to embrace me, but I step back. I thought my emotions had calmed enough but the anger from yesterday is beginning to rear its head once more.

"How could you have not said anything? I've been here for months. You knew I was here but still you didn't say anything. And then my grandmother dies... and still nothing," I ask, staring at her coldly. I see the sadness and frustration reflected in her own eyes before the crease between her brow draws together.

"I wanted to so many times." Her voice shakes slightly. "She was my grandmother too. I lost her too, Amelia. I didn't want you to go through this alone, but how was I supposed to tell you all of this? You've had so much on your shoulders, I didn't want to add to it," she says, staring at her feet.

"She's not lying and she is family," Kylah says.

"Family wouldn't have hid themselves from me," I reply, still feeling the sting of loss so acutely I don't know how to move forward with this. *"She could have reached out earlier. I could have used her sooner."*

"She's here now," Kylah insists.

Leave it to my panther to point out the obvious.

"How do we move forward from here?" Reid asks,

looking around. "I'm assuming you need to keep your cover as AJ for as long as possible. And Nathaniel, where do you fit in all of this?"

"This is insanity," Sir speaks up from where he's been silently listening. "How are you going to accomplish anything with the state our world is in? Rani needs to pay for what she's done, and you kids need to be protected."

"Brother, I hate to break this to you, but they aren't really kids anymore. Not after all of this. Amelia is going to be queen soon," Nathaniel stares at his brother.

"You're right, but they still need to be protected. Now I understand why you think the prophecy is real. Amelia Huntsman you may find yourself in a very strange situation indeed," he says, staring at me with his piercing eyes.

"It can get stranger than all of this?" I ask, waving my arms around.

"Truth is often stranger than fiction dear girl," he smirks. His face completely changes with this small gesture. The harsh angles of his face soften, and I can see something of a kind person peeking out.

It dawns on me. This man is my uncle!

"Wait. He's your brother and my dad, so you're my uncle." I stare at him with my jaw dropped open.

"Astute observation," he chuckles.

"Who are you and what have you done with Sir?" Spence asks, staring at him with wide eyes.

"I hazard to guess I would have been a nicer man had my life gone differently," he replies, his eyes glazing over in thought until he shakes his head. "Regardless, I am committed to helping this cause however I can."

"It might mean breaking some rules, brother. And we all know how you feel about rules." Nathaniel elbows him.

"Well yes, but I believe the rules are about to change so

we are in uncharted territory," he clears his throat, shifting on his feet uncomfortably.

"Can we have lunch brought here?" I ask my mother. "I think we all need to discuss everything to do with the prophecy, why the panthers went missing, and what you found out about Queen Rani."

"That's an excellent idea." Sir nods in approval.

Demetria nods as she pulls out a vial and downs it. Before long AJ is standing in front of us and takes off to get food for our impromptu lunch.

"Let's start with the history of the prophecy," Sir clears his throat. We all sit forward to listen as he speaks. "When it was first brought to us by the witches, they said it would change shifter society as we know it. As it was circulated around, a group called the Radicals rose in opposition to the thought of change. Panthers were slaughtered in an attempt to prevent it from happening, until the Radicals were dismantled by the crown. The panther population took significant casualties, but with a time of peace their numbers began to grow again."

"So, the Radicals nearly wiped out an entire line of royals?" Kenton asks, his eyes wide.

"Very nearly, son. Over the years a new group calling themselves by the same name would pop up and attack the panthers, but they were always wiped out quickly before much damage could be done. By the time Queen Adrielle took the throne, the panthers were thriving and had quite a large royal family. She herself had four daughters and several granddaughters. When Queen Rani took the throne, the Radicals resurfaced again. It appeared by all accounts that the Radicals were being dealt with, but the royal family quickly lost numbers. No matter what the queens were doing to fight the threat, each princess was systematically eradicated until only Demetria was left," he says. "When she took off, we thought it might end the panther line. Then reports of hidden princesses popped up. But you're the only one who survived the trip back."

"Jack said the queens ordered their executions," I reply.

"Sounds like Jack needs to talk to Queen Calyope about that. Because my grandmother ordered they all be brought back," AJ says from the doorway. "Lunch is on its way."

We mill around until our lunch arrives and then we dig in, making idle small talk until we finish. Once the empty dishes are taken away, AJ reaches in his pocket and drinks another vial and morphs back into Demetria.

"What other questions do you have?" she asks.

"What have you collected on Rani?" I question. "After seventeen years, surely there's something."

"Our biggest issue is she was good at keeping everything removed from herself. She used her chain of command to keep the orders so separated we had no proof to tie back to her. Until she went after you with her own beta then after the other queens. She finally got bold enough to crumble the entire thing. She would kill her own supporters if they were caught before they could be questioned. Claiming swift action to protect the panther princesses." Demetria's eyes cloud over as her jaw ticks.

"What about my fathers?" Kenton asks quietly. "How involved are they?"

"We are still trying to determine that. Best case scenario they were actively ignoring her wrongs, and at worst case they were active participants," she answers.

"I need to talk to them. I want to hear the truth from their own mouths," he says as he clenches his hands to his sides.

"We can do that, but don't jump to conclusions. They aren't speaking at the moment. Maybe they will want to answer you," she says softly.

"That's a good idea," I agree, feeling emotionally spent. So much is going on in our lives right now, but we need to let Kenton get the answers he needs.

Demetria removes a blue bottle from her pocket and downs it. We all watch with rapt fascination as her body stretches and morphs back into the familiar AJ.

"That is so weird," Dom says.

"Try experiencing it," AJ or Demetria says. "Who do you want to join you, Kenton?"

"I think it would be best if it's only Lia for now. They might not talk if we come as a group," he answers, looking at the rest of my mates.

"Fair enough," Dom nods.

We say goodbye to Nathaniel and Sir, then AJ leads us to the cells where his fathers are being held.

"I can give you some privacy, but we will be listening from here," he says.

"Thank you," I meet his eyes.

We walk through the door leading to their lone hallway and a shiver runs down my spine.

"Kylah, do you sense anything?" I ask, looking around.

"The one on the right," she answers.

I turn to look at the man glaring at me from his cell. His black hair shining in stark contrast to his icy blue eyes. Kenton's eyes follow mine and his lips form a thin line when his eyes land on the man.

"Why are you looking at my mate that way, father?" he asks through a clenched jaw.

"Your mate? Hardly. She's panther scum who's going to murder your mother," he spits.

"Gerald, what is wrong with you?" the man across from him asks, his face wearing a mask of horror.

"Don't be so naive, Luca. You're always trying to see the good in everyone. But really all this child is here to do is incriminate us. His little *mate* has decided you're all guilty and trying to find the proof," Gerald snarls.

"But the only guilty one is you, Gerald, isn't it?" I ask, staring him down.

"I don't have to admit to anything," he sneers.

"Luca, isn't guilty. Rani hid it from him," a voice pops in my head.

"Who is this?" I ask, looking around when my eyes land on a blonde man that resembles Kenton.

"Pablo is what you may call me. Luca and Triston were her idealist. They couldn't see past their love for our mate. Gerald is the only active participant," he explains.

"I'll let you speak to your fathers alone," I grab Kenton's hand and squeeze it. "Let us know if you need us."

I knock on the steel door and step out when it swings open. I pull AJ aside and tell him what they told me, hoping it will help, then wait for Kenton to join us. He spends a few more minutes in there before he comes storming out.

"Gerald needs to go on trial next to my mother. He's her henchman," Kenton's jaw ticks. "Why is my family so fucked up?"

"I'm so sorry." I rush forward and wrap my arms around him.

"It's not your fault. I just... I don't know anymore," he sighs.

"I understand." I lay my head against his chest. "But I'm always here if you need me.

Queen Calyope is waiting for us when we get back.

"Amelia. How are you? It must have been a huge shock to meet your father," she wraps her arms around me as soon as she's close enough.

"How did you know about that?" I ask, my eyes going wide.

"I sent one of the guards to tell her," AJ says, clearing his throat. Man, it's weird to know that it's really my mother there.

"Oh, that makes sense," I reply. My brain isn't working very well right now, so many thoughts and no time to process any of them.

"If you need to talk, I'm always here for you. We have a big day tomorrow. The trial needs to be organized and it's going to be interesting. Ava will sit in for her mother, since she's still out of commission and you will sit in for Adrielle," the leopard queen explains.

"I'll do whatever you need of me," I assure her. "I think I'm going to go ahead and skip dinner and go to bed."

"Get some rest, and if you need anything just ask," she says.

She let's go of me and I make my way back to my room, the guys on my heels. I plop on the bed as soon as we arrive and lay back. How am I going to get through what's coming?

"Trouble, how are you doing, really?" Kenton asks as he sits down next to me.

"I'm confused, angry, sad, and numb. I don't know how to process any of this," I reply.

"That's understandable. I feel a lot of that myself," he sighs and lays back next to me.

"Aren't we a mess?" I chuckle.

"Why don't we all change, and we can relax together for a while?" Vance offers.

"You're my new favorite," I sit up and a small smile lifts the corner of my lips as tears slide down my face. I'm an absolute mess. What would I do without my mates?

"Lia, if any of us were in your position, we would be needing you right now too. Just let us take care of you until you can take care of yourself," Vance says walking forward and kissing my forehead.

"You're right. Thank you, all of you. I'm so glad to have found you all," I sniffle.

I get up, collect my pajamas, then go in the bathroom and change. When I get back to the bedroom, the guys all look more comfortable in their pajama pants and loose shirts.

"I'm glad this bed is big enough for all of us. Want to lay down and watch TV?" I ask.

"I get to lay next to Lia!" Vance yells and jumps on the bed.

I giggle and crawl in next to him, while the others wrestle to get the spot on the other side of me. Kenton breaks through the pack first and flops down next to me. He grabs my hand and earns a smile. As long as these guys are with me, I know I can get through anything life throws at me.

"Jet, wake up," Reid shakes my shoulder.

"Five more days," I groan and pull the pillow over my head.

"While I would love to spend a week laying around with you, unfortunately, you have other responsibilities that can't wait," he replies.

"I know; I know," I sigh and sit up, wincing at the bright light streaming through the window.

I crawl out of the now empty bed. Where is everyone? Reid sees the look on my face.

"They are making breakfast. You looked so peaceful we wanted to let you sleep as long as possible," he says.

"I guess I really do have to get up then," I sigh. I feel selfish, but I'm not ready to face all that's to come.

I know as soon as I walk out of this door reality will be waiting. The trial for Kenton's mom.

I slip out of bed and go to the bathroom to shower, getting ready for the day. I just need a few minutes to turn my brain off and think about nothing before reality slaps me in the face.

After I'm dressed and ready to face the day, I make my way into the kitchen. My guys are sitting at the table with Queen Calyope's husbands.

"Lia! Sit down. Are you hungry?" Vance jumps up when he sees me.

"I could eat." I give him a small smile.

Vance pulls out a chair for me and I sit down as he pushes my chair under me. He lays a kiss on the top of my head before he sits back down. Reid places a plate of biscuits and gravy in front of me and my stomach growls. It smells so good I dig in.

When the queen joins us, I notice Rachael and Jack aren't present.

"Where's Jack and Rachael?" I ask, looking around.

"I sent them away until everything is settled. I'm not going to risk my grandchild with all this foolishness. If she was here, she would be required to compete in the queen trials, pregnant or not," Calyope explains. "We have to lower the age this year to make an exception for you and that puts her in as well."

"I wish I could have said goodbye," I sniff.

"I'm sorry, Lia, but I had to sneak them out without anyone finding out. As soon as the new queens are crowned they will be back," she gives me a sad look.

"I understand, but it still makes me sad," I reply as I put my dishes in the sink. "I have a question though, how do the trials work?"

"That I can answer easily. The queens already have their throne. For someone to replace them, they have to compete in the trials to prove they have what it takes. If they pass the first three then they get to stand up and prove they are more dominant than the current queen, they are going for. If they are more dominant, then they take the throne; if they can't make the queen kneel, then the queen keeps her throne until the next trials," she explains. "It will work a bit differently this year, but we will figure it out."

"We have our first meeting after lunch so you have free time this morning," Queen Calyope says.

"Thanks," I reply.

"Trouble, can I talk to you?" Kenton asks, nervously shifting back and forth on his feet.

"Sure, what's up? I ask.

He grabs my hand and leads me back to the bedroom. I sit on the edge of the bed as he paces back and forth in front of me.

"I want to go see my mom, to confront her," he finally says. "And I want you to go with me."

"I mean, whatever you need to do, but why do you want me there?" I ask, seething at the thought of seeing that horrid woman.

"To prove to you that my allegiance is to you and always will be," he stares me in the eye.

"You don't have to prove anything to me, but if you want me there with you, I'm happy to support you," I reply as I stand up.

"I need you there," he says quietly.

"Let's grab De… AJ and go," I reply.

I don't want any part of this, but I need to be there for Kenton. If he needs this, then it's the least I can do. We find AJ in the living room and tell him our plan.

"Are you sure this is a good idea?" He gives Kenton a strange look.

"I have to do this," Kenton bunches his hands at his sides.

AJ shrugs and leads us out of the apartment through long winding hallways until we reach the holding cells. We pass by rows of normal cells until we come to a heavily guarded thick steel door. Kenton stops in his tracks and swallows hard, as if he's having second thoughts about this. I reach out and squeeze his hand to remind him that I'm here with him and he moves forward again. AJ speaks in a low voice to the guards in front of the door, and when he finishes, they move and let us pass.

I gasp as Queen Rani comes into view. She looks like a smaller, disheveled version of herself. Did this pathetic woman really orchestrate everything?

"Kenton! Did you come to clear my name?" Her eyes light up when she sees him.

"No mother. I came to tell you to your face how horrible I think you are. To go after my mate and her family… How could you?" he growls, his eyes brimming with pain.

"It's all just a misunderstanding. Surely you don't believe those people," she tsks.

"Of course I believe my mate. Have you forgotten you CALLED me and tried to force me to leave her after you had her poisoned?" he screams.

"Well, I… You see…" She tries to find the words to answer his accusation but fails.

"Save it for the trial. I just needed you to know that I will always choose Lia. She's my mate and I don't care about you," he growls. I can feel his lion just under the surface, attempting to assert dominance over his mother.

I cover my mouth with my hands when she kneels. How the hell did she become queen when her own son is more dominant? Men in our community are never stronger than queens.

"I can feel him pulling from us," Kylah says.

"What do you mean?" I ask.

Kenton walks out without looking back. I'm so shocked, I scramble to catch up. I need to ask AJ about this as soon as we are alone. I don't need anyone overhearing this conversation. Kenton is silent the entire way back. I hold his hand, but he feels miles away. I'm sure it was hard to confront his mother like that, but I don't know how to help him.

When we arrive back at the leopard queen's suite, I pull AJ and Kenton back to my room to get to the bottom of this. The other guys see us come in and follow as well.

"Where did you guys disappear to, and why does Kenton look like someone kicked his cat?" Dom asks.

"We visited his mother in her cell; he can tell you what he wants of the rest," I answer. "AJ, how is Kenton more dominant than a queen?"

"I'm guessing he's borrowing some of it from you," AJ answers.

"He can do that?" My eyes open wide.

"It's been documented in mated pairs in the past. If one is extremely emotional, they can borrow from the other," AJ explains. "I've never experienced it. I've just read about it."

"That actually makes a lot of sense," I nod my head. "Kylah said she could feel him pulling something from us."

"Do we have to wait until after the trial to get out of here and do something?" Spence asks. "I want to take Killer on a date."

"Sorry, you'll have to wait until we make sure Rani's dead first. We can't take any chances with Amelia," AJ gives him a sorry look.

AJ leaves the room and Kenton recounts the meeting with his mother to the guys. I don't know how to feel about the entire thing. I'm so glad that he chose me and made a public stand on it, but I feel horrible that the bitch put him in this situation.

"Do you think your brother will come home for the trial?" I ask, realizing I've still never met him.

"Not sure. My mother was never his favorite person, but I don't know that he would want to see her die." Kenton shrugs.

"Why does life have to be so fucked up?" I ask as I flop back onto the bed.

"I don't know, but hopefully once they crown the new queens, all of this will blow over and we can just live our lives," Dom replies.

"You realize that unless I fail the trials I'm pretty much guaranteed a crown on my head right?" I ask. "I don't think things will ever be normal again."

"I never said normal, Kitten. I said live our lives. That means in whatever form it comes. I'm with you no matter what." He lies on the bed next to me and kisses my forehead.

"I think you are all forgetting that Lia could be the cat the prophecy is about. She might be the only queen when this is over," Reid points out.

"I'm trying to ignore that for now." I give him a pointed look.

"You'll still have us with you. It doesn't matter how this all plays out." Spence walks forward and kisses my forehead.

"I'm so happy I have all of you. Can you believe I was scared to have five mates? Now I think the universe knew I would need you all just to get through this life," I chuckle.

"I just can't wait until we can take you out and treat you like a real princess. Take you on dates, spoil you rotten. All that good stuff," Spence says.

"I'm happy as long as you're with me. I don't need stuff to feel loved. All the little gestures tell me every day how much I mean to you. I hope you guys know how much you mean to me," I reply.

We spend the next couple of hours relaxing, talking about nothing. The guys do their best to keep my thoughts preoccupied so I don't worry about what's coming. When lunch time rolls around, a pit forms in my stomach. What comes next is going to suck so bad. We have to get everything set up for the trial, and I feel like a fish out of water. I eat as slow as I possibly can, trying to delay the inevitable.

"Amelia, you can't put this off any longer. I'm sorry, sweetie," Queen Calyope says.

"I was hoping." I give a half-hearted smile.

I get up from my seat and Reid grabs my plate, taking away my last procrastination tool. I follow Queen Calyope out, and we make our way to her study where Ava is already waiting.

"I'm sorry you girls have to step into these rolls this soon, but we can't wait for Queen Sierra, and Amelia you would have been stuck with this regardless. I called for this meeting to explain how this works so you'll be prepared. The trial will start tomorrow morning. Both sides will present their evidence then we are expected to provide a verdict immediately. If Rani is found guilty, she will be sentenced to a public execution. Do you have any questions?" she asks.

"So, we act as judge and jury?" I ask, my eyes widening.

"We do." She nods.

"Can we ask questions?" Ava asks.

"If something isn't clear, you can ask them to clarify, but we are supposed to be impartial, so random questions are discouraged," Queen Calyope explains.

Ava nods and we sit and chat until we understand what is expected of us.

CHAPTER FOUR

The next morning, my stomach is in knots. We are deciding the fate of Kenton's mother today. After breakfast Queen Calyope gathers Ava and I in her study to speak again before the trial.

"We have a last minute change. We are trying Gerald, Rani's husband, at the same time. The defense asked to defend them together when charges were formally announced yesterday," she explains.

"So it's all or nothing? They are both innocent or guilty?" I ask.

"No. We can decide separately," she explains. "It's time to go."

Ava and I follow Queen Calyope to the far end of the castle into a courtroom. We enter from the back and take our seats behind the raised podium. The seating on the main floor and balcony is completely full, but it's eerily silent, as if everyone is afraid to talk.

Rani is brought out with her hands and feet cuffed together and the crowd starts booing immediately. I didn't know how hated the lion queen was, but this is very telling.

"You're letting children decide my fate?" she shrieks when her eyes land on us.

"Silence!" Queen Calyope booms. "You know the law Rani."

Rani is seated at the table to the left and an older gentleman joins her. A few minutes later Gerald is led out and seated on the other side of Rani. Another man sits at the table to the right and the trial begins.

"Rani and Gerald Huntsman, you have been charged with treason for the murder of Adrielle Huntsman and the attempted murders of Seirra and Calyope Huntsman. How do you plead?" Queen Calyope asks.

"Not guilty," they say in unison.

"That's the prosecutor, Mr. Finch," Queen Calyope whispers.

Mr. Finch stands up and addresses us.

"Queen Rani and her husband Gerald are accused of treason. I will prove beyond a reasonable doubt their guilt," he says, making a show of his short speech. "The prosecution would like to call a witness to the stand."

The steward that was captured is dragged to the stand in handcuffs, his eyes darting around nervously.

"Please tell us your name," Queen Calyope says.

The steward's eyes grow wide when they land on her. "Raymond Price," he answers.

The prosecutor begins asking him pointed questions and the man's story begins to play out.

Gerald approached him personally with poison and a dagger to take care of the queen he served under. They threatened his life and that of his family if he didn't comply.

I begin to feel bad for the traitor as I hear his account of things, but he still chose to carry it out instead of going to another queen to report it.

When he's dismissed, Mr. Finch presents two bags

containing evidence he wants to submit to the court. We look over the murder weapon and the poison that Queen Seirra was given.

He also passes forward statements from Rani's other husbands indicating they knew nothing of her actions, but that Gerald's cat had admitted their guilt while confined.

When he's finished, he takes a seat. The man sitting next to Rani stands.

"That's the defense, Mr. Longfellow," Queen Calyope whispers.

"Just because a lowly steward claims that my clients approached him doesn't make it true. The poison or dagger could have come from anywhere. Why would a queen attack her fellow queens? She says she didn't do it, that's enough for me," he smiles then sits back down.

"I want to speak for myself. This lawyer is useless!" Rani shouts from her seat.

I look over to Queen Calyope and she just shrugs.

"We'll allow it," I announce, hoping I did that right.

"Stupid children running a court. What's next a child queen?" Rani mutters under her breath.

I ball my hands into fists but keep my face calm.

"Did I want my son away from the mockery of a panther princess? Yes, I did. Did I hire a witch coven to create a toxin to do it? Again yes, but I didn't know it could kill her. I didn't actually kill anyone with my own two hands so you can't find me guilty." Rani smiles and sits back down. "You can't prove I had anything to do with the poisoning of one queen or the murder of another."

"So, to clarify, the toxin that Amelia Huntsman was injected with was formulated just for you?" Ava asks. Crap I had forgotten that's the same toxin her mother was injected with.

"That's correct. I had the only supply known to man," Rani confirms.

The prosecuting lawyer smiles and stands up. "Exhibit M. The toxin that Queen Sierra was poisoned with proves to be the same as the one Amelia Huntsman was injected with," he says, bringing a report to the podium.

I open the report and the analysis of the toxin used on me and the one they found in Queen Sierra are identical. She was so ready to brag she admitted her own guilt.

"Wait! I didn't mean that. I meant..." Rani stutters.

"I told you to keep your mouth shut," her lawyer shakes his head.

"You weren't defending me," she replies.

"I was doing the best I could with what I had," he sighs as he crosses his arms across his chest.

"The prosecution rests," the younger lawyer smiles.

"Rani Huntsman, do you have any last words for the court?" Queen Calyope asks.

"I think I've said all I need to," she holds her chin high.

"In that case we will retire and come up with our verdict. Take a fifteen minute recess," Queen Calyope says then stands up.

Ava and I follow her lead and we make our way to a small office behind the podium.

"She's clearly guilty and shows no remorse; do we even need to have this discussion?" Ava asks, pacing in front of the door.

"The public needs to view us as making a calm and informed decision. We gave her enough rope and she hung herself. She knows the outcome; they know the outcome, but we need to appear to be taking everything into consideration. That's why it's only a fifteen-minute recess," the queen replies.

"I guess that makes sense," Ava deflates.

"What about Gerald?" I ask. "They focused more on Rani than him. I think he's guilty as well, especially with the statements from Rani's other husbands."

"I agree. Do you feel it's enough to find him guilty?" Queen Calyope asks.

"I do," Ava nods.

"Do we need to decide anything else?" I ask.

"Only the method of execution," Queen Calyope answers.

"What's customary for treason?" I ask.

"Public hanging," she replies.

"Then we should do that. Treat her the same as anyone else who would commit treason. Let everyone know nobody is above the law," I reply. "Gerald can hang at the same time. It will show swift and just action."

"Lia, you really will make a great queen," Ava stares at me with wide eyes.

"I agree, and that's the perfect solution. The people will respect us because we aren't showing her any special treatment," Queen Calyope nods. "Time is almost up, let's go tell the verdict. Amelia, I would like you to make the announcement. It will grind Rani's gears."

"I can do that," I reply, but inside I want to shrink up and run away. This will be the first time I address my people. The first time I have to hand down a sentence. I feel like I have to prove I can do this.

We enter the courtroom and take our seats behind the podium again. The room is silent and full already. It's as if no one bothered taking a break. I guess they wanted to know the verdict too badly to risk it. Queen Calyope nods to me so I stand up and clear my throat.

"Rani Huntsman and Gerald Huntsman, you have been found guilty of treason. You will be sentenced to public hanging at the end of these proceedings," I say, trying to sound as professional as possible.

Rani jumps out of her seat and a guard rushes forward to subdue her. "You're going to execute me like a commoner?" she shrieks as she's forced back in her chair.

"You committed the crime; the laws are absolute. It doesn't matter your station. *You* break the law. *You* receive the punishment," Queen Calyope responds. "Now take them away."

The crowd erupts in cheers as Rani and Gerald are dragged out of the courtroom to their fate.

"Are they really going to hang them now?" Ava asks.

"Yes, AJ has asked for the privilege of being their executioner," Queen Calyope answers. "We need to get out there. It's customary for us to witness the death of those we bring judgement on."

My stomach drops. It was one thing sentencing someone to death, but another thing entirely having to witness it. Am I strong enough to do this? It doesn't really matter. I have to be. This is my life now. I take a deep breath and stand up. Queen Calyope watches me carefully.

"Are you sure you are up to this Amelia?" she asks.

"It's a part of the position. It doesn't matter how I feel about it, what matters is that I woman up and do it," I reply, meeting her eyes with mine.

"I don't know if I can do this," Ava whispers from the other side of Queen Calyope.

"Yes you can. You are in a difficult position, but when the going gets tough, we have to get tougher," I say firmly.

"How can you pretend this isn't making you sick to your stomach?" she asks.

"I don't know. It sucks, I don't want to do it... but I feel like I would be letting people down if I gave into my own insecurities. I just have to get through this one moment then I can go home and lose my shit in private," I explain.

"I think I can do that. Just get through it, then fall apart…" she nods.

"Let your brother help you pick up the pieces, unless you've found your mates?" I suggest.

"I haven't yet." She gives me a sad look.

"Then let Marc help you. We all get by with a little help," I say.

"Amelia Huntsman you are wise beyond your years, dear girl. Now we've lingered too long. We need to take our places," Queen Calyope says.

We follow her outside to a courtyard that's filled with people. The gallows are sitting prominently in the front. Four raised seats are placed front and center. Every fiber of my being wants to run away back to my room and hide from this harsh reality.

"You sentenced them so you need to witness what that means," Kylah says.

"I know, and I know they're guilty, but I've never witnessed someone die," I reply.

I continue walking confidently, trying to appear like this is something I was prepared to do. I catch a glimpse of my guys in the audience and my heart breaks. No matter what she did, Kenton shouldn't have to watch his mother die. I want to go to him, to tell him he doesn't have to do this… but I know that he wouldn't listen.

"Kylah, please talk to Kenton. He shouldn't be here," I plead.

"Yes, he should. No one can question his loyalty now," she argues.

AJ approaches the gallows from the right side and climbs the stairs. The crowd goes silent.

"Rani and Gerald Huntsman have been tried and convicted of treason. Their punishment is death by hanging," he announces.

Rani is walked up to the gallows, fighting at her chains

the entire way. A noose is slipped around her neck and tightened. She begins pleading for her life, but it falls on deaf ears.

"This is why the panthers needed to die. Look at what they are doing to me," she screams, looking half-crazed.

Gerald is walked up next to her, remaining silent.

AJ leans forward and whispers something into her ear, causing her eyes to bulge, before placing a burlap sack over her head. He does the same to Gerald then steps away to a wooden lever. He gives her one last look then pulls on the lever and the floor falls out from underneath Rani and Gerald at the same time. They fall with a sickening crack as their necks are snapped.

The crowd erupts in cheers when it's finished. I find it cruel and sickening. We just watched someone lose their life. Granted, she was an evil bitch hell bent on killing everyone else… I guess I can't blame them for cheering.

"Show's over, clear out," AJ calls as the guards take Rani's body down.

"You can go now," Queen Calyope says.

Ava wastes no to beelining into the castle. I look around, but the guys aren't where I left them. I wanted their security before I left my seat, instead AJ is at my side.

"They are almost to the throne. They got pushed back by the throng of people leaving," he says.

"Oh, how did you know?" I ask.

"It was all over your face, princess. You will be an amazing queen after what I've witnessed today," he says.

"Thank you," I reply. I'm still not sure where my relationship with this person, my mother, is.

The guys reach me and AJ escorts us back to my original room.

"We can be here again?" I ask, looking around confused.

"So far we haven't found any more of Rani's people. You having her killed as a commoner destroyed any illusion of power she had left so the rest would have ran for the hills," AJ says as he pulls out a vial and drinks it.

Suddenly Demetria is in front of me again, wrapping her arms around me.

"I'm so sorry you had to go through all of that. You handled the trial and hanging with the dignity of Adrielle herself," she gushes.

"Now that Rani isn't a threat, are you going to come back as Demetria?" I ask.

"Not until the trials are over. I was never meant to be queen. It's not in my nature, but you were made for it," she replies, smiling at me proudly.

"So, after I'm crowned as queen, you are going to come back as yourself?" I ask, wanting to hear her say it.

"As soon as that crown is on your head, I will be back as your mother, if you will have me," she looks down at her feet, her eyes glistening with unshed tears.

"I honestly don't know how I feel about you or Nathaniel yet, but I do want the chance to get to know you both. Everything has been happening so fast, I just haven't been able to think about anything," I say.

"That's more than I could hope for," she nods.

"So... does this mean we can take Lia on dates yet?" Spence asks with a cheesy grin.

"As long as you take security and don't leave the island, I think it will be ok in a couple of days. Let's let things settle down first," she raises an eyebrow at him.

"Bollocks," he says.

"Bollocks?" I ask.

"He's trying to swear in British today," Dom rolls his eyes.

"What's it mean?"

"Balls," the guys say together.

"Spence, you can be so strange," I shake my head and smile.

"Hey, I resemble that remark," he grins back. "But at least I made you smile. Your eyes looked haunted."

I take a deep breath. I'm not ready to break down. Today was harder than I thought it was going to be. She tried to kill me… she had my grandmother killed, but it was still hard to watch her die. It didn't make me feel better; it just made life feel senseless.

"Can you tell me what to expect from the trials?" I ask Demetria.

"They will test your intelligence, willingness to work as a team, strength, and dominance. There will be four tests to pass and if you fail even one, there will be no panther queen until the next trial," she explains. "The first three trials change, but the last trial is to show your dominance over the current queen. If you are more dominant, you become queen. If she is more dominant, she keeps her throne. Since there is no panther queen, I'm not sure how they are going to test that for you."

"This sounds doable," I reply.

I pace back and forth nervously. Winter break has come to an end peacefully and it's time to go back to school. That means seeing Nathaniel more often and I don't know how this is going to go. He hasn't reached out to me. Does he even want to be in my life?

"You ready to go, Trouble?" Kenton asks from my open doorway.

"Ready as I'll ever be," I reply.

On one hand, I can't wait to get out of this castle, but on the other hand, I'm dreading returning to school. Rachael won't be there, and I have Nathaniel there. It's strange to think of having a birth parents after thinking they were dead. At least I have the guys, and Ava and I have grown closer since the trial. So much has happened since then. We learned Queen Sierra died the day after the trial. Ava was beside herself, but she's found solace in our late-night talks. Her mother's funeral was four days ago. For some reason, the cure that worked for me, didn't touch Queen Sierra.

I follow Kenton out to the car and take a last look at the castle. It's not changed in appearance, but now feels different. It's become a home, a place of loss, a place of joy, and so many other things. It's hard to believe how much my life has changed in these short few months. We get in the car and pull away, driving back to where it all started.

There hasn't been that much time that has passed from the time I first came to the Huntsman Academy, but to me, it could have been decades. So much has changed. I arrived here a naive girl, with no knowledge of her history or family, no knowledge of how this world ran, and the trials I faced between Amy and her bunch... the threats and that poor dead cat.

Things are different now. I'm no longer naive to this life and somewhere along the way, I gave up being a kid. Now that things have changed, I've made my peace with who I once was. I've made peace knowing that I'll never be that girl again. I've made peace with what I've learned, with the passing of my grandmother, and with the death of Rani. Today is a new day for me. A new day to learn more about this world, to prepare for the trials I'll be facing, to figure out my relationship with my parents, and the five guys that have stuck by me through every second of this whirlwind

"A penny for your thoughts, Trouble," Kenton says.

"You'd need lots of pennies," I half-heartedly chuckle.

"I'll settle for the biggest one," he replies.

"Oh, that's a loaded answer. Just everything that's happened since Jack showed up. Going back to school after this winter break seems surreal. Like all of that happened, and now back to school. I don't feel like a kid anymore I guess," I sigh.

"You aren't a kid anymore. None of us are. But rules are rules," he shrugs. "Want to know the funniest part; when you are crowned queen, they will still probably force you to go to school."

"That's just weird," I giggle. "But accurate. Rules are in

place for a reason. Besides, I need to learn this stuff, especially if I'm expected to rule."

"That's why you are going to be an amazing queen," Kenton says.

"People keep saying that," I mumble.

"Because it's true," Kenton nods firmly. "I've lived in the castle with good and bad queens," his light brows furrow for a moment. The events of the last months passing through those blue eyes before he shakes his head freeing himself from his own thoughts. "You will be one of the good ones... the best one."

"I just hope I don't let anyone down," I sigh.

"You could never let me down," he says quietly.

We arrive at the academy and it somehow feels less foreboding than I thought it would. We take our small amount of luggage up to our rooms then the guys all come to mine.

We hang out on the couch watching movies until Spence stands up and clears his throat.

"I've been really patient considering everything has been batshit crazy, but Amelia Huntsman, will you do me the honor of going on a date with me this Friday night?" he asks, kneeling on one knee.

"I would love to Spence," I giggle at his formality.

"What about the rest of us?" Vance asks, raising an eyebrow.

"He did ask first," I shrug.

"Fair point. We should have a game night. Winner gets the second solo date with Lia," Dom suggests.

"Oh, that sounds like fun!" I clap my hands.

"Good, we'll arrange everything, Kitten," Dom smiles.

We finish the movie, and its nearly time for lights out. As the guys are getting up to leave, there's a knock on my door. Who would be visiting this late? Assuming it's Ava, I rush forward to open the door myself and come face to face with Nathaniel.

We stare at each other without speaking. I'm so shocked to see him, and his eyes look pained.

"Amelia, I don't know how to do this, but can we talk?" he asks.

"Sure, come on in," I step out of the doorway.

"Do you want us to stay, Trouble?" Kenton asks.

"No, you can go. I think this needs to be a private thing. I'll call if I need you," I smile at him.

"If you're sure," Dom says, eyeing Nathaniel.

"I'm sure. Thank you all for everything though," I reply.

The guys leave and I'm left alone with my birth father for the first time. We stand awkwardly silent for a few minutes.

"Do you want to sit down?" I ask.

"Yeah, sure. I'm so sorry, Amelia. Maybe I'm not ready yet," he sighs as he sits on the couch.

I sit down next to him.

"Ready for what?" I ask.

"To interact with people. I somehow pulled it together for the funeral, but when we got back, I let Leo take over again. I've spent a few hours a day in my human form with Heath-cliff, trying to adjust," he explains.

"We need to stay protected. Feelings hurt," Leo growls.

"Our human sides need each other," Kylah insists.

"We only need each other. I protect him from the bonds that could chain us," Leo insists.

"Then you are the one hurting him," she growls.

My eyes open wide and I understand now. He was so busy trying to learn how to be a person again, he didn't have time to talk to me. That's why I didn't hear from him again.

"It must be really hard," I say.

"I should have never let myself get like this. If I would have known you existed… I would have never let you grow up thinking you weren't wanted," he says as a tear slides down his cheek.

"If it makes you feel better, I grew up thinking I was a bear, and I had a very loving family. I didn't even realize I was adopted until my first shift," I left out a self-deprecating laugh.

"I know your mother had her reasons, but she still kind of fucked us both over. The damnedest thing though, I still love her," he says.

"She is your mate, that kind of makes sense. Seeing her again... Did it make your mate bond come back to life?" I ask.

"It did, which makes all this harder. I want to just forgive her, but I'm so angry at her. It's warring in my chest," he sighs. "Sorry I didn't mean to unload this on you. I meant to come here and ask if you were even interested in getting to know me."

"I'm already getting to know you. I'm genetically half you. As for the rest, sometimes it's easier to talk to someone you don't know well yet. And we are in the same boat. We both thought she was dead and then boom there she is," I reply. "I'm not sure what to think about it yet, but I'm going to keep an open mind. I don't think she took any of her decisions lightly. I'm sorry she hurt you so badly."

"That's what makes me the angriest. She hurt me, but she left you. I understand why she did it. Hell, if our roles were reversed I can't say I wouldn't do the same. It just sucks to be the other party. Then I think about how it had to have hurt her too. She feels things deeper than she lets on," he explains.

"I can't say what I would do. I would want to keep my baby safe at all costs... but I don't know if I have the balls to hurt my mates," I reply.

"Your mother has more balls than the rest of us

combined," he laughs. "I've never seen a woman resist a mating bond like she did."

"So, where do you want to go from here?" I ask.

"I want to be whatever you need me to be. I missed out on so much and I really hate that. But I understand you already have parents," he says, his voice breaking in pain.

"Yes, I have parents who love me, but love is infinite. There's nothing saying I can't have another dad," I reply, trying to comfort him.

"You really would be willing to explore that?" he asks, his eyes hopeful.

"If you are open to it, so am I. We didn't know about each other before now. Why should either of us be punished for that?" I ask.

"Amelia, you really are an amazing young woman," he looks at me with awe on his face.

"It's going to take me time to learn to be a person again. Please be patient with me. I need to go. Leo wants to run," he says abruptly, standing and bolting from the room.

Wow, that has to be one of the strangest, most beautiful conversations I've ever had. I get ready for bed and sleep well for the first time in weeks.

CHAPTER SIX

"Let's move the couch against the wall," Dom says, grabbing one side.

"Why are you rearranging my furniture?" I ask.

"We're playing Twister," he grins.

"Spence breaks out a poster board with a tournament bracket on it. I'm not sure how they have this set up, but games sound fun.

"We will play a different game each night, and tally up who has the most wins by Friday. The winner gets a solo date next week. Saturday we are going to go out as a group," he explains.

"What's the bracket for?" I ask, not understanding.

"To determine who wins Twister," Dom says.

"Let's play Rock, Paper, Scissors to see what order we go in," Vance says.

We play several rounds, until Dom and I are the last two standing.

"Looks like Lia and I are first," he grins.

"Wait, what happens if I win the game tournament?" I ask.

"They we get another group date," Kenton says. "We were

going to say then you get to choose, but I figured you wouldn't want to."

"You're right. It's too hard to choose," I sigh in relief.

Vance grabs the spinner. "Get ready you two," he says and spins the dials. "Right hand green."

We both put our right hands on green. This is easy so far.

"Right foot yellow."

"Left hand red."

This continues on, until Dom and I are tangled up together.

"Sorry, Kitten, but I'm playing to win," he says with a mischievous glint in his eyes.

"Left hand green," Vance calls out.

Dom's hand shoots up and tickles my ribs causing me to lose my balance and fall.

"Not fair," I laugh.

Spence writes Dom's name as the winner of our match and the next two take their places. We continue in this manner until only Dom and Kenton are left.

We watch as they twist and turn, both refusing to let the other win. We stop using the dial and start calling out combinations, trying to trip one of them up. The next time a hand is called, Dom tries to tickle Kenton like he did me, but Kenton is ready for him and smacks his hand away. Who knew twister could be such a competitive game?

"Right foot green," Spence calls out, then winks at me.

The two are tangled in such a way when Dom tries to move his foot they both topple over.

"Guess we will have to call it a draw. You both get a win on this one," Spence says.

"Man, I thought you guys were never going to finish," Reid says.

"They are the most competitive ones," Vance replies. "It's not surprising."

We clean up from Twister and put the couch back in place. After classes all day, and our game night, I'm more tired than I thought I would be, but I'm not ready to give up time with my guys. I settle in between Vance and Spence while we watch *Supernatural*. I end up dozing off and wake up in my bed with my alarm blaring the next morning.

I get up and rush through my morning routine so I can get breakfast. When I arrive in the sub-level commissary, I'm shocked to see Nathaniel sitting at one of the tables.

I grab my food and sit across from him. I don't know what compelled me to come down here alone, but for once I'm glad I did. This isn't what I expected to find.

"Kylah, can you let the guys know where I am?" I ask.

"I can," she yawns.

"Thank you," I reply.

"How are you doing, Daddio?" I ask, sounding lame to my own ears.

He cracks a smile. "Daddio?" he repeats.

"I was trying to be funny; it didn't come off right," I cover my face with my hand.

"I appreciate the effort. And to answer your question, today is a good day. Leo and I came to an agreement. He understands we need to rejoin society and he's agreed to give me control back. Let's see how long his resolve last," he chuckles.

"You listened to what I said," Kylah purrs.

"You made sense. I shouldn't hurt him. He needs this bond with his child," Leo replies.

"That is good news!" I exclaim.

"I'm surprised to see you without your entourage," he comments.

"Kylah told them where we are. I'm sure they'll be here soon. So, what do you plan to do with your life now that you're mostly back on two legs?" I ask.

"Since I was in the enforcers, I'm hoping to get a job as a guard. That way I can be closer to you," he replies.

"I heard AJ has a soft spot for shaggy lions," I tease. "I bet you could talk him into a job."

"This is going to be so weird," Nathaniel shakes his head.

"It's not so bad. Just try to think of them as separate people. It's what I do," I say around a mouthful of food.

"She reeks of magic. I don't know if I can do that," he mumbles.

"Why can't I smell it?" I ask.

"Not sure. Maybe it's because Leo was in control for so many years," he shrugs.

My guys come in the commissary and I wave them over.

"Hi Nathaniel," Vance smiles.

"Um, hello," he says, his eyes darting to the exit.

"Do crowds bother you?" I ask.

"They do. I know I need to get over it, but it's been a long time…" he says, still staring at the door.

"Go, we can talk again later," I tell him.

"Thank you, Amelia. I'm trying…" he says as he gets up and rushes out the door.

"At least he's on two feet. That counts for something," Dom says, placing a hand on top of mine.

"It counts for a lot," I agree.

The guys grab their food and we eat a quick breakfast, before a long day of class. Kenton and I head off to our shifting class. As soon as I walk into the locker room, Ava pounces on me, giving me a big hug.

"Girl, I've missed you," she says as she squeezes.

"You know where my room is. You're always welcome to stop by," I chuckle and hug her back.

"I thought about it, but I didn't want to interrupt your time with your mates," she says as she let's go, looking down at her feet.

"None of that now. You are always welcome, period. Yes, hanging out alone with my mates is awesome, but I will always make time for my friends," I tell her firmly.

"You really mean that," she looks at me cocking her head. "A lot of people say things like that, but they are empty platitudes. But you are so different, Lia."

"I think I'll consider that a compliment," I laugh.

"It really is," she nods.

"We're having a game night, if you want to join tonight. I'll tell the boys to behave but I doubt they will. Whoever wins their little game tournament gets the next solo date with yours truly," I explain.

"Oh, now I really want to see this. Um, can Marc come too? He's shut down a lot since Mom…" she trails off.

"The more the merrier. It should be interesting to say the least. Last night was Twister, who knows what they have planned for tonight," I giggle.

"Thank you, Lia. I mean it. I don't know what I would have done without you. Sorry I was such a bitch in the beginning," she says, guilt heavy in her eyes.

"Don't worry about it. We can't change the past, but we can always make our present the best it can be." I reach out and squeeze her hand as we exit the locker room.

CHAPTER SEVEN

We all meet up in my room when classes are over. I already warned the guys Ava and Marc were joining us, and they didn't bat an eye. I'm so thankful I have such amazing mates.

Dom comes in with a large whiteboard and the other guys laugh as he wrestles to set it up.

"What do we need that for?" Ava asks when she arrives with Marc in tow.

"We're playing Pictionary." Reid grins.

"We'll split into two teams of four and compete. The winning team gets a point towards date night with Lia," Vance explains.

"Spence should be on a team with Lia, Marc, and Ava. He's already getting a date and they don't need one," Kenton says.

The other guys agree, but Ava speaks up. "What if I want a date with Lia?" she asks, raising an eyebrow.

Dom growls, Kenton falls over laughing, and the others stare at her with a shocked expression on their faces.

"Do you want a date with me, Ava?" I ask.

"No, I just wondered what would happen if I did and we won," she winks.

We split into our teams and start playing. The guys go first with Dom drawing. They can't guess what he's drawn so we have a chance to steal.

It looks like a shark swimming with a boat and an island in the distance.

"Jaws!" Marc blurts out.

"Aw man. How did he get that and the rest of you couldn't?" Dom throws his arms up in the air before erasing the board and sitting down.

"Good guess, Marc," I encourage him.

"Thanks," he gives a small smile that doesn't quite reach his eyes.

"Lia, you draw first," Spence suggest.

"Ok, but I can't draw my way out of a paper bag," I warn them.

I draw a card and it says family. Well crap. *I'm the last person in the world to define that,* I think to myself.

"You have more family than most. Family is what you make it," Kylah reminds me.

"That was smart," I reply.

I draw a tall stick figure, then a slightly shorter stick figure and add long hair to it. Then I draw two short stick figures.

"Parents," Ava calls out.

"Kids," Spence says.

"Family," Marc says quietly.

"Marc got it again," I say then erase the board.

"I think we should have picked Marc for our team," Vance grumbles.

I stick my tongue out at him.

We play a few more rounds and the score is tied up, and it's my turn to draw again. I don't like this pressure. I walk forward and draw a card. Wow, it couldn't get any easier than this, now hopefully I can draw it. The single word written on the card is cat.

I do my best to draw a small cat on the board.

"Oh, it's a cat!" Ava shouts. "That means we win!"

"Dang it," Kenton says, still smiling.

"I'm starving, can we go eat now?" I ask, checking the time.

"Let's go feed Killer," Spence chuckles.

We all exit my room and start making our way to the commissary, but Sir stops me on the main floor.

"Amelia, I need to have a word with you and Ava in private," he says.

"Is everything all right?" I ask, a lump forming in my throat.

"Yes, everything in fine. It's nothing like that," he says, turning around and walking towards his office.

I let out a sigh of relief as I follow.

"I'll catch up with you guys when I'm done," I say over my shoulder.

Sir doesn't say another word until we are seated in his office with the door closed.

"Queen Calyope called this morning and the arrangements for the trials have been made. Typically, students don't participate, but given the unique circumstance we are in, all royal female students will also be required to attend. You are the only two left in attendance at the moment," he explains. "I still don't think it's right, but I understand the necessity. Ava, you can fill out a petition to defer to the next trials if you would like, but Amelia, you are the only panther available, so you don't have that option."

"How long do we have to prepare?" I ask, hoping my voice sounds confident, because inside I'm falling apart. I knew this was coming, but it seemed like a far-off thing, especially once we got back to school.

"Two months from tomorrow," he says quietly, looking at his hands.

"How do I fill out the deferral paperwork?" Ava asks, then glances at me. "I'm not ready for this."

"I don't blame you," I smile at her.

"Meet with me tomorrow and I will help you fill it out. Damn shame that children have to compete in royal trials now," he shakes his head. "As for you Amelia, Nathaniel and Mz. Payne have both agreed to work with you to get you ready for what you might face. You are excused from your other classes until this is over."

"Thank you, Sir," I reply.

"In private you may call me Uncle Heathcliff, if you like," he offers.

"That might take some getting used to." I grin.

"Yes, it might." He smiles back. "Go get something to eat. Sleep well tonight, Amelia. Your training starts tomorrow."

Ava and I leave his office and my head is spinning. One more month of semi-normal life. Except for the whole training nonstop for royal trials. I don't know how I managed to fool myself that I could go back to being just a normal teenager for a while. It was never going to happen.

"I'm sorry, Lia. I know I should stand with you, but that trial... I'm not ready for this shit," she shakes her head.

"Don't be sorry. You shouldn't be forced to go early because they had to change the rules for me. I'm glad you get to stay safe and be normal for a little longer," I smile at her. "Besides I need someone to cheer me on aside from those mates of mine. They will be too busy worrying."

"Isn't that the truth," she chuckles.

We make our way back to the commissary and grab our

trays before joining the rest of the group. When we sit down, we are assaulted with questions. Now doesn't feel like an appropriate place to answer, so I let them know we will talk in private. Kenton crosses his arms across his chest, but the others accept the answer and continue eating. As soon as we are finished, we say goodbye to Marc and Ava then head back to my room.

I go over everything Sir told me, and what is expected of me in the coming weeks. It becomes more real, relaying the information to them. In a few short weeks, if everything goes in my favor, I will be a queen.

"I can't believe you have to go through this so young," Kenton paces back and forth. "The next trials weren't supposed to happen until after we graduated."

"We already knew it was going to happen. Coming back to school just made it seem farther away somehow," Reid says.

"Kitten can do it. She's stronger than anyone gives her credit for," Dom says.

"Thanks for the vote of confidence." I smile at him.

We settle in on the couch for a few hours, just hanging around and chatting until I decide to turn in. I know the next two months are going to be exhausting, so better sleep while I can.

I wake up to a loud knocking at my door. I glance at the clock and it's only five in the morning. What is going on? I stumble out of bed and answer the door to Nathaniel standing there.

"Get dressed in comfortable clothes then meet me in the commissary. Training starts now," he grins mischievously.

"Why so early?" I yawn.

"Have to start building your endurance up. We don't have much time, so you're going to be working long days. Sorry kiddo." He shrugs.

"I'll see you in a few." I shake my head, trying to clear the fog as I close the door.

I grab a pair of yoga pants and a soft t-shirt then run into the bathroom. I quickly get dressed and pull my hair back before digging out a pair of sneakers.

Running down the steps, I'm worried I took too long to get ready when I don't see Nathaniel sitting anywhere. I grab food from the station that's open this early and eat quickly, wondering where I should meet him. I could have sworn he said meet him here.

A few minutes later he comes walking through the door, his eyes wide in shock when they land on me.

"I figured it would take you longer to get ready," he says when he approaches.

"You told me to hurry so I hurried," I say around a mouthful of eggs.

"You can slow down a little," he chuckles. "I thought it would take you longer to wake up and get down here."

"Well, you better get to eating then old man. I'm almost finished." I raise an eyebrow at him.

"You are definitely your mother's daughter." He grins then walks off to get his food.

When he returns, I say, "I'm going to assume you meant that as a compliment."

"Always, Amelia," he says softly.

"So what was life like for you growing up?" I ask, wondering how to broach the conversation of his family.

"I was raised in the noble community. It was mainly Heathcliff and I against the world. Our parents were always gone, trying to save the world," he rolls his eyes.

"Are they still alive, your parents?" I ask.

"They are. They moved away from the island when I went feral. You'd have to ask your uncle if he's talked to them. I haven't seen them since I came back," his eyes darken. I decide to drop my questions for now.

We finish eating in silence then make our way outside. The air has a chill to it, but not biting cold like where I grew up.

"So, what are we going to work on?" I ask.

"First, we are going to run in our human forms," he says then takes off jogging.

I take off and catch up, and we speed up to a brisk pace, making laps around the school. I develop a stitch in my side after a while and start to slow down.

"Run through the pain," he grunts.

I push forward, focusing on putting one foot in front of the other. When did I stop doing this so frequently? I used to run every day, and now I can't remember the last time I got up for a morning run. I'm kind of glad this is a part of my training. Now that I'm doing it, I find that I've missed it.

We run past the pain and I hit a state of almost euphoria. This is my favorite part of the run. You feel great, like you can do anything. I don't get it every time I run, but when I do, it makes it so easy to lose yourself to it.

Nathaniel slows down to a jog, and I match his pace as we continue to slow down until we are walking.

"Why are we stopping?" I ask.

"Amelia, we've been running for three hours," he gives me a worried look.

"Oh, I lost track of time." I blush.

"I can tell you've been a runner," he chuckles. "At least I know we can push you on this. Now, Mz. Payne has time for you so go see her. She wants to work with your shifting."

"Sounds good. Thanks for the run," I say. "Wait, where do I meet her?"

"At the training field. And grab some water," he reminds me.

I run inside the commissary and grab a bottle of water then make my way out to the training grounds where Mz. Payne is waiting.

"Amelia, I'm so sorry you have to go through all this," she says when I get close.

"It's life." I shrug. "Can't change it, so I need to meet it head on."

"Truer words have never been spoken," she nods, pride shining in her eyes. "Let's talk about the trials for a few minutes. I want to tell you about what they faced in the last trials, so you will have an idea of what you could face."

"That makes sense," I nod.

"The last trials consisted of four parts. There was an obstacle course to be completed in cat form. Then they had a hand to hand combat section in human form between contestants. The third was an endurance race and the last trial is always the same. You have to prove your dominance over the reigning queen. I'm not sure how that's going to work with Queen Calyope being the only standing queen at the moment, but I guess we will see."

"So are the trials always the same, or can they change?" I ask.

"I've only witnessed one trial so I wouldn't know for sure. But we are going to plan like they are a possibility. I think they would test the same characteristics no matter the form of the trial," she replies.

"Where do we start?" I ask.

"Go ahead and shift and we will work on obstacles. Nathaniel will work on these with you when I have classes to teach," she says.

I strip out of my clothes and let Kylah come forward. I'm a bit nervous about this training, but I don't want to complain. The only way to go forward is to go through it.

"We can do this," Kylah says.

"And if we can't, we will learn," I reply.

I follow Mz. Payne, who's also shifted through the woods to a small clearing where several obstacles have been set up.

"My name is Trina," her tiger purrs in my head. *"I'll demonstrate the first one then you try."*

She approaches a tall, thin tower. It doesn't look like anything should be able to climb its smooth surface. I walk forward then pace around the structure, looking for places to dig my claws in, or something. I give up and sit down and watch as Mz. Payne continues looking at the structure, her tail flicking.

She backs up then runs forward and leaps, wrapping her front paws around the tower. I look up and notice it's more textured a quarter of the way up. I would have never noticed that on my own. I'm really going to have to learn to think outside the box and take in all of my surroundings.

She slowly crawls up the tower onto the platform at the top then sits and stares at me. Guess it's my turn. I get up and examine the tower closer. The texture is different on each side, starting at higher and lower points. I finally choose the side I want to attempt and then move back and run towards it and leap. I try to dig my claws in but they just scrape at the smooth surface and I slide back down. Damn, she made it look easy.

I shake myself off and try again, getting the same result. My tail flicks rapidly with my growing frustration.

"What if the texture on the other sides is an illusion?" Kylah asks.

"Wait, I didn't think about that," I reply.

We circle back to the side we watched Mz. Payne crawl up and run and jump and bingo, our claws sink in and we are able to pull ourselves up.

"Good job, you saw through the deception," Trina says. *"You need to get lunch then go back to work with Nathaniel."*

"Thank you, but how do we get down?" I ask.

"Jump," she says, then demonstrates.

Here goes nothing. I jump and we land softly. I take off back to the first clearing, shift back, then get dressed before heading to the commissary. I'm just getting my food when I feel my mates walk in. It's strange going so long and not seeing them. I've been spoiled with their time lately. We sit together and chat. I explain what my training consists of, and they complain about boring classes.

I want to sit longer, but when I see Nathaniel poke his head in the door to the commissary, I know my time is up. I give hugs to all my mates before sprinting out to meet with Nathaniel.

"What are we doing next?" I ask, already feeling tired from the day's activities.

"Running again. Have to build up your endurance first," he says.

I sigh but start jogging, letting him catch up with me this time. We speed up and he pushes me faster and faster this run, until we are flying around the perimeter. My energy is waning, but I push until my legs shake and I trip forward and fall.

"Amelia, are you ok?" Nathanial says from above me.

"I'm sorry. I tripped," I say as he helps me up.

My legs are shaking as I stand.

"Damnit, I pushed too hard. Why didn't you say something?" he asks.

"I was trying to keep up. I only have two months," I reply, trying to keep my balance.

"I think your electrolytes are out of balance," he mutters scooping me up and rushing me into the school.

He takes me to the nurse's office an lays me on the cot. The nurse checks me over and gives me Gatorade to drink.

"If you're going to push her this hard, keep her drinking this," she tuts at Nathaniel.

"You're right. I messed up." He pulls on his hair.

After downing the bottle, a few minutes later, I begin to feel better. The nurse hands me another one and tells me to keep sipping on it.

"You're done for the day," Nathaniel says. "We can't push you any further without keeping you down."

"Are you sure?" I ask, not wanting to get behind. I have so little time to train.

"Amelia, we ran for seven hours today," he says. "That's

more than I expected to get today, and I still pushed too hard."

"You're just trying to help. I don't mind hard work," I try to reassure him.

"Go eat dinner and get some rest. Tomorrow we are going to work on your combat skills," he says, then takes off out of the nurse's office.

"Stay hydrated and eat more. You need calories to work the way he's going to push you," the nurse says before dismissing me.

I take off out of the nurse's office and make my way to the commissary where I find my mates already eating.

"What game are we playing tonight?" I ask, trying to stifle a yawn.

"Are you up to playing games?" Dom asks, his eyes piercing through me.

"I think so," I reply.

"Trouble, you forgot to get food," Kenton reminds me.

"Oh, right," I yawn again.

I didn't realize how drained I am. I start to get up, but Vance places a hand on my shoulder.

"I'll get it for you," he says then takes off to grab me a tray.

"What did you do all day?" Reid asks.

"Ran a lot and tried to complete an obstacle in cat form," I answer.

"Why don't we just relax this evening? You need to rest if they are going to be working you this hard," Spence suggests.

"Then who wins a date with me?" I giggle.

"We can totally keep the competition going on our own," Spence raises the corners of his mouth in a mischievous smile. "Besides, I want you well-rested before our date on Friday night."

Vance returns with my food and I scarf it down before we

head back to my room. When I open the door, I'm shocked to see AJ waiting on the couch.

"What are you doing here?" I ask, not sure how I'm feeling about this invasion of my space.

"I came to see you," he replies. "If it's a bad time, I can come back later."

"It's fine. What do you need?" I ask as I make my way to sit down next to him, my mates hanging back by the door.

"I wanted to know how you were doing. I know you've had a lot thrown on your plate, and I want you to know I'm here for you," he says.

"When I'm alone with my guys, it's like I can pretend life is back to normal. Then I have to wake up and start training and reality sinks in again," I admit, trying to stifle a yawn.

"Do you need help with training?" he asks, concern in his eyes.

"Nathaniel and Mz. Payne are training me," I reply.

"If you need anything from me, all you need to do is call," he says.

"Thank you for that," I smile. "I would love to talk more and get to know you, but I can barely keep my eyes open."

"Go to sleep, Amelia. Soon we will have time to really talk," he says then stands up and leaves.

The guys who had hung back by the doorway join me on the couch, and I end up falling asleep before they decide what to watch.

CHAPTER NINE

The week moves forward in the same manner. Running, obstacle, running... building my endurance and trying to think outside the box enough to get me through the trials without failing. Although I hide it the best I can, the pressure is a lot. So much rides on me getting these trials and coming out the other side the Panther Queen. I've been so focused on training that my time with the guys has begun to dwindle little by little, but it's finally Friday, and I'm more than excited for my date with Spence.

"Can we stop a little early today?" I ask Nathaniel as we jog around the grounds.

"Why?" he asks, giving me a strange look.

"Because I have a date with Spence, and I feel like I'm neglecting my mates," I reply. "My chest is starting to ache."

"That's a good reason. We will stop when classes let out and take tomorrow off, but your ass is back in training mode on Sunday," he replies.

"I can still run with you Saturday morning," I offer.

"Only if you want to, kiddo," he grins.

"I need to be ready. I can't afford too much time off," I sigh.

"I'm glad you have a good work ethic, but time off is important too. You have to let your body recover," he reminds me.

We stop at a clearing in the trees towards the back of the property. If we hadn't been using it all week, I would have never known it was here. We work through basic defensive and offensive maneuvers. The same ones, over and over again. I've yet to even touch him once, but my reaction times are slowly improving. I wish I had longer to prepare, because I'm afraid I'm going to get my ass handed to me in this portion of the trials.

"Keep your knees bent," Nathaniel barks. "Straighten your shoulders."

I do as he says and adjust my stance as he runs the same drills over and over again. I just want to be able to catch him off guard once.

"Go for his left knee," Kylah whispers.

"Why? That's not what we are doing," I reply confused.

"He favors it. Think outside the box," she sighs.

I school my face to hide the small smile that tries to form on my lips. The next time he lunges forward, I kick out my leg and sweep it into the left knee and he falls over.

"Not what we were working on, but I'll take it. Always look for your opponent's weaknesses. Your cat will notice them quickly so work as a team," he says as he gets to his feet.

"She suggested taking you down when I was getting frustrated," I admit.

"Trust those instincts. We can work on muscle memory and proper form. but those instincts are what will make it or break it in a fight," he explains.

"I'm terrified of failing," I admit.

"You won't fail. You were born for this," he replies adamantly.

We break for a quick lunch then I work with Mz. Payne for the rest of the afternoon.

I've managed to complete three obstacles out of the six she has set up. I'm nervous about the new one we are approaching. It's a single, thin pipe stretched over a bed of sharp spikes. Along the pipe, there are places where heavy logs swing, spikes shoot up from the ground, and a strange vine wraps around a portion. This is the most dangerous one we've looked at yet.

"Are they trying to kill us?" I ask.

"Trying to thin the weak from the running. None of these should kill you, in theory. But they could cause some nasty injuries. We aren't going to try this but study how it works. Once you see a way through the course, then we will change it and study it again. The main takeaway is to learn how to evaluate a safe path," she explains.

"When will I attempt it then?" I ask.

"You'll try it when you're ready. Don't rush headfirst into a situation without evaluating all possible outcomes. A good leader thinks through their options without rash decisions," she raises an eyebrow at me. "Most of the women in these trials have been training for years."

We walk around the course while she explains each component and what will happen when it's triggered. My head is swimming by the time we are done.

I rush up to my room and get ready to go out with Spence tonight. I have no idea what he has planned, but I want to look nice for him. I take a quick shower, do my makeup for the first time in a week, and then fix my hair. I can't decide what to wear. Standing in my closet, I go over everything and really wish Rachael was here. Maybe she'll come back now that she can defer out of the trials.

I settle on a pair of tight black jeans, a one shoulder purple top, and my kitten heeled boots. As I exit the closet, someone knocks on my door. I answer it to find Spence grinning at me holding a bunch of daffodils.

"These are gorgeous, but I don't have a vase to put them in," I say, taking the flowers from him and bringing my nose close to smell them.

"Yes, you do. I dropped it off yesterday. You were just too tired to notice," he grins as he steps into the room and grabs a bright turquoise vase sitting on the table by the couch.

He fills it up with water and adds a packet of plant food, and I add the flowers before setting it on my nightstand.

"What are we doing tonight?" I ask, butterflies jittering around in my stomach.

"It's a surprise. Let's go," he smiles and grabs my hand.

We go downstairs and out through the front door to his car. He opens the door for me then closes it once I'm sitting down before running around and getting in himself.

We head towards town, then continue on through until we drive out the other side again. The houses spread out until we are surrounded by woods. The trees gradually thin out and we find ourselves on a white sand beach. I've been here for months, and never even thought about visiting the ocean. My life has been way to crazy.

"Wait here, please," he says as he gets out and goes to the trunk of his car.

The sun is starting to set on the horizon in front of us as Spence opens my door.

"Ready, Killer?" he asks.

"What do you have up your sleeve?" I grin at him as I get out.

"Spoilers," he winks.

He leads me down to the beach where a black and white plaid blanket is spread out with a picnic basket sitting in the middle. I sit down and watch the sunset as he lights torches around the blanket.

"It occurred to me that we never brought you here. I love watching the sunset and stargazing from this little beach," he says softly.

"It's beautiful," I reply as he sits next to me.

I settle into him as he wraps his arm around my shoulder and we silently watch as the sky darkens, and the stars start twinkling to life. The moon is full and bathing us in its light as Spence starts unpacking the basket.

"I didn't know what you would want to eat, so I just brought some finger foods," he says, biting his bottom lip.

"Anything is perfect when I'm with you," I reply, leaning forward and catching his lips with mine.

He forgets about the food and moves forward, until he's on top of me and I'm lying flat on the blanket. The kiss deepens and my stomach clenches.

"Lia, we have to stop, or I won't," he whispers, resting his forehead on my own.

"What if I don't want you to stop?" I ask, out of breath.

"There's too much at stake right now. We can't add this into the mix," he says, his eyes close.

"You're right, but I don't like it," I sigh.

He slowly lifts himself off of me and returns to the food. He fills up the plates with cheese, crackers, meats, and grapes then we chat while we eat everything he packed.

When we finish, we pack away the dishes then lay back and cuddle together while we look at the stars.

"This is where I come when I need to think. It feels like I'm alone with my thoughts out here," Spence says. "I wanted to share this with you so you could always have somewhere quiet to go if you needed to."

"Thank you. It feels like my problems are worlds away

right now. I needed this more than I realized," I squeeze him tight.

"Anytime, Killer. We would all do anything for you. Just don't forget to lean on us. We miss you," he says, his voice taking a serious tone.

"I miss you all too. Training is crazy right now, and I have to work my hardest. I can't fail," I explain.

"I'm going to talk to the guys, but why don't we train with you? At least when we can. I doubt Sir will let us all out of class to help," he offers.

"That would be awesome. It wouldn't hurt to have more motivation," I chuckle.

"We better head back to school. We already missed lights out," he says reluctantly.

"Just five more minutes," I say, not wanting to lose this feeling.

CHAPTER TEN

The next morning, I wake up before my alarm. I pull on my work out clothes and head out the door where I run into Reid.

"Why are you up so early?" I ask as we walk down the stairs.

"We're going to take turns running with you in the mornings," he says.

"Breakfast first. I can't run on an empty stomach," I grin.

We head down to the commissary, which is empty save for the staff.

"No one gets up early around here, huh," Reid says when he looks around.

"It's usually just Nathaniel and me," I confirm.

We grab our food and sit down when Nathaniel walks in. He sees Reid sitting with me and cocks his head but doesn't say anything. He grabs his food and sits on the other side of the room.

"Why didn't he sit with us?" Reid asks. "Does he not like me?"

"I can hear you talk about me you know," Nathaniel says.

"I didn't sit with you because I didn't figure you wanted me to."

"Oh, well, you're welcome to join us," Reid clears his throat uncomfortably.

"Reid is going to run with us this morning. The guys want to participate with my training," I tell Nathaniel as he makes his way towards us.

"That's wise. Your mates should learn to fight," he nods his head.

We finish eating and begin jogging around the school on our normal path. About an hour into the run, Reid starts falling back further and further. I'm torn between slowing down so he can keep pace and pushing myself to run faster.

"They all need to be out here running twice a day. I'm going to talk to my brother about excusing them from classes. They need more work than you do," Nathaniel shakes his head. "Push through the pain, boy. It will only get worse before it gets better."

"How… do… you… talk…" he huffs out, trying to keep up.

"It's all about building up your endurance," Nathaniel shakes his head, but a small smile forms on his lips.

We slow down to a jog and end our run early. I'm scared Reid is going to pass out. His face is bright red, and he's having a hard time catching his breath.

"I want all of you out here tomorrow morning for a run. Tonight, as well if you can manage it," Nathaniel says.

"But we are supposed to take Lia bowling," Reid says when he catches his breath.

"Then I guess you'll be running before you go bowling. Lia, I promised you the day off so you can sit it out," Nathaniel replies.

"I can run again. It's still spending time with my mates," I grin.

"That's my girl," he smiles widely, showing his teeth.

Reid and I head back to our rooms, and I text the rest of the guys, letting them know what Nathaniel wants to do before crawling back in bed for an overdue nap.

I end up sleeping until early afternoon. I check my phone and realize we are set to run again in a few minutes. I drag myself out of bed and get ready to head out. I send a quick text telling the guys I'll meet them downstairs and start stretching my tired muscles.

I leave my room and sprint down the stairs where the guys are all waiting for me.

"You ready for this?" I ask, grinning.

"I warned them that you guys are beasts." Reid shudders.

"We aren't that bad. I used to run every morning before I moved here. I didn't realize how much I missed it until I started again," I explain.

"Then we will make sure you get to run even when things are hectic," Kenton says.

We make our way through the school and meet Nathaniel at the back.

"This is the one and only time I'll take it easy on you," he warns then starts jogging.

I catch up quickly without saying a word and can feel the others fall into step around us. Nathaniel increases our pace until we are running, though slower than normal. I start inching forward, wanting to fly, but hold myself back for the guys. I don't know if any of them could keep up.

Dom pulls forward and matches me stride for stride. I accept his challenge and before long we are in front of the group, the distance increasing with every stride.

"I didn't know you were a runner," I say.

"I used to before we came to school. I don't know why I stopped either. I want to run with you, Kitten." He grins.

We run like this until Nathaniel catches up to us.

"We're going to slow down and stop now. I think those guys have had it." He points over his shoulder.

I glance back and the rest of the guys act like they want to fall over. Dom and I slow down until they catch up and continue to slow our pace until we are walking.

"How do you do this every morning?" Kenton pants.

"You're about to find out." I smile sweetly at him.

"Why did we sign up for this again?" Reid asks.

"Because we want to help Killer," Spence replies. "Let's go get cleaned up so we can have some fun. No wonder she's been falling asleep on us."

"This was a short run. Wait until tomorrow morning." Nathaniel shakes his head and walks off.

"Is he serious?" Kenton asks, his eyes widening.

"Yup," I reply as we turn and walk inside.

As soon as I reach my room, I jump in the shower and get dressed to go out with the guys as a group tonight. We are going to grab dinner in the commissary then go bowling.

The guys start arriving in my room then we all go down to eat together. We hurry through our meal, excited to finally go out and have some fun together.

"Trouble is going to ride with me," Kenton announces as we head outside.

"Then I'm riding with you too." Dom grins.

"Me too," Vance volunteers.

"Looks like your stuck with me," Spence tells Reid.

"We need a bigger car," I shake my head.

"Maybe you should get an SUV with third row seating," Kenton says.

"I never thought about getting a car. I always ride with you guys," I say as we pile into the car.

The ride into town is short, and we pull up outside of the bowling alley, which announces its name in bright pink neon letters.

"Really? The bowling alley is just called Bowling Alley?" I ask.

"It is the only one on the island. I guess they never bothered giving it a different name," Vance says.

We spend the rest of the evening throwing balls at the pins. Stealing little touches and caresses between turns. When they announce the lanes will be closing soon, I'm sad for the day to end. It was nice to escape and feel like a teenager for a moment.

CHAPTER ELEVEN

The weeks fly by, training nonstop at a grueling pace. Every day my guys subject themselves to the same routine, never complaining at all. In the evenings we relax together until it's time to sleep so we can wake up and do it all again.

Today is the last day of training. Nathaniel and Mz. Payne want me to take tomorrow off to rest before the trials the next day. I can't believe it's almost here already. It feels like we just started. AJ has been coming out to help with my combat training. It's been nice to work through some of my anger towards my mother, but the tension between him and Nathaniel makes it awkward at times.

I head down the stairs and meet the guys and Nathaniel for breakfast. I'm starting to think of him as my dad, but I don't know how he would feel about me calling him that.

We start off with a short run after breakfast, then break into groups and work on our hand-to-hand. I've managed to take down everyone but Nathaniel and today is my last chance.

We face off while the others watch. Kylah is sitting just

below the surface, watching his every move. He tenses like he's going to move right but goes left instead, almost catching me off guard.

"Watch his eyes," Kylah hisses. *"They always dart at where he's going."*

I pay attention to his eyes, and sure enough, they are his tell. I cut him off on his next attack and sweep his feet out from under him then sit on his chest.

"I win," I say proudly.

"Took you long enough," he chuckles as I move so he can get up. "I think you are ready."

"As ready as I'm going to be," I agree. "Thank you, Dad."

"Did you just?" he asks, tears welling up in his eyes.

I nod my head yes as he wraps his arms around me in a tight bear hug.

"I'm so proud of you, daughter," he says. "I've been dying to say that."

The guys and I head back to our rooms to get ready to return to the castle. I'm nervous about what the future holds, but there is no delaying the inevitable.

A car comes to pick me up. The guys want to ride with me, but I convince them to drive so they don't have to leave their cars here. When we pull up to the castle, I thank the driver as he holds the door open for me to get out.

As soon as I walk through the front door, Kylah gets excited.

"Our family is here," she purrs.

I survey the area for who she is talking about and squeal when I see Rachael and Jack coming down the corridor. I run forward to meet them and wrap my arms around both of them.

"I've missed you so much," I say.

"We've missed you too, Lia," Rachael says, hugging me tight.

"Your belly is growing," I say when she let's go and see the perfectly round bump that's forming. "When did you get back?"

"Last week, but my mother wouldn't let us contact you. She was afraid it would distract you from your training," Rachael says sadly.

"How are you doing, Lia? You ready for all of this?" Jack asks.

"As ready as I'm going to be. I'm so glad to see you both. Did I say that already?" I grin.

"Close enough," Jack chuckles.

The guys all arrive, and we head back to my room and catch up with Jack and Rachael. We fill them in on everything that's happened from meeting my father, my mother being alive, and what happened at Rani's trial. They tell us about staying on the island with Davina and the witches until Queen Calyope called them back.

"Where is AJ? I'm shocked we haven't see him," Vance points out.

"My mother has him busy setting up for the trials," Rachael replies. "He's the lead guard for the castle so he's in charge of it too."

"I was hoping we would get a chance to talk," I stare down at my hands.

From our training sessions together, I've grown closer to my birth parents and find myself wanting to spend time with them. I was hoping being at the castle would give me more time alone with my mother, even if she appeared as AJ, but I guess duty calls.

We join Queen Calyope and her family for dinner. It's so surreal to think that in a couple of days, I will either be a queen or fail. But failure isn't really an option. There's no one else to fill my spot if I do. Talk about pressure.

After a dinner full of idle chit chat, the guys and I make

our way back to my room to relax. It all just feels like the calm before the storm. I wish I had training tomorrow to take my mind off of waiting. Time feels like it's dragging on slower and slower, the closer it gets. I fall asleep at some point on the couch, surrounded by my mates.

The next morning, I wake up to someone knocking at my door. I crawl off of the couch, trying not to wake anyone up. I guess everyone decided to just crash where we were.

When I open the door, AJ's smiling face greets me. I move to the side so he can enter. As soon as I close the door, he pulls out a vile and changes back to Demetria.

"Amelia, how are you?" she asks, wrapping me in a tight hug.

"I'm good. Just tired of waiting and full of nervous energy," I admit.

"Do you have any questions about what happens?" she asks.

"If I do win, what happens?" I question her.

"When you win, you'll be crowned right after. Things move fast in the clan. They want everything cemented quickly," she explains.

"You are so confident in me," I reply.

"You were born for this," she smiles. "We can go for a run. The plans are ready so I took today off to spend it with you."

"No running," Reid calls out from the couch. "I can't run anymore."

"Who would have thought he would turn down a chance to let his cat out," Demetria's laugh tinkles across the room.

"That's a different story," Reid says. "But how do you hide your panther?"

"AJ isn't a panther shifter. When he shifts it's a tiger," she shrugs. "It's magic. I can't explain it."

The guys get up and Demetria takes a second potion to transform back into AJ.

"That's my last switch to Demetria until the trials are over. I only have one left," he says, his eyes downcast.

"Then let's go run and leave our problems here for a while," Vance says.

We follow AJ through the castle to the back where there's a tall, fenced area.

"This is where we shift to burn off some steam," he explains as he opens the gate.

Once we are inside, it's set up as a jungle area with tall trees and winding paths disappearing into their depths.

We quickly strip off our clothes and shift before taking off down one of the trails. We run and play, those of us who can climb do so as we just enjoy the moment and freedom only shifting allows.

After a while we make our way to the beginning and shift back before getting dressed.

"Thank you. I needed that," I tell AJ.

"I didn't realize you guys could shift for that long already at your ages. They must be training hard with you. I believe you can do this, Amelia. I'm so proud of the woman you've become," he says.

"I just hope I don't let everyone down," I reply.

"You could never let us down, Jet." Reid wraps his arms around me. "You are more than enough no matter what happens."

When we get back inside the castle, we run into Queen Calyope.

"Lia, I was looking for you. I've had your uniform for tomorrow delivered to your room. We need to be at the trial grounds by nine tomorrow morning," she explains.

"Oh, thank you. I'll be ready," I reply.

"You'll do great," she smiles at me.

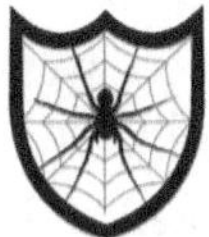

CHAPTER TWELVE

The next morning, I get up and dress in my uniform for the trials. It's a sleek black robe over black t-shirt and black yoga pants. At least it's practical for what's to come.

I grab a quick breakfast with my mates then head to the trial grounds, just beyond the castle. It's a cool morning, the wind gently blowing and the sun shining brightly overhead. As we approach, the stands are already filling up with people. It looks like the entire island has come out to see who the next queens will be. Not surprising, but a little bit intimidating.

Nathaniel suddenly appears in front of us. I need to focus; I didn't even see him coming. Not good.

"Stop worrying, Amelia. You will do fine. The prophecy has been leading us all to this moment," he wraps me in a hug for the first time.

"I've been meaning to ask, what witches did you ask about this?" I ask.

"When I was in the enforcers, I questioned a few. The prophecy is the same as we were taught. One panther will reign. You have the right mates and the situation is set up for you to win," he winks.

"We will see," I sigh. "I'm a little bit overwhelmed. These other women have been training for years…"

"But you are dominant and smart and capable. You will blow through the trials, and when it's over, I'll say I told you so," he grins before walking off.

"He's right, Trouble. You were made for this," Kenton leans forward and kisses me.

"Get out of your own head and kick some ass," Dom grins before kissing my forehead.

The rest of the guys show their support and give me hugs before making their way to the stands. I walk to where the other women are waiting and join them.

"Fake confidence. Don't let them underestimate us," Kylah warns me.

There are fifteen other women here, which surprises me. I somehow assumed it would be more. Queen Calyope steps out and joins us holding a microphone.

"Thank you all for coming out to show your support. The trials are an important part of our selection process. We want only the brightest and best leading our community. Today we will find out who has what it takes to be our next rulers.

"There are four trials our contenders must face. Trial number one is the hand to hand combat portion. A queen needs to be able to defend herself and her people from threats. Each participant's name was entered into a lottery and drawn at random for their pairings. Sixteen brave contenders will begin this trial but only the strongest will advance to the next round," Queen Calyope explains. "AJ will pair up the opponents and you will begin on my mark."

AJ steps out names two at a time until we are all paired up. We stand, ready and waiting for Queen Calyope's command. Once the go ahead is given, I begin sizing up the petite tiger in front of me. Her dark black hair is up high in a bun, and her blue eyes are fierce as they seem to penetrate through me. I wait for her to make a move, watching for her weakness.

She charges forward, and we grapple, each holding the other at bay. She gets over on me, shifting her weight to flip me across her body. I land hard on my side and feel the air knocked out of me. Quickly she's on top of me, but I shift before she can secure her hold on me, flipping her off me and onto the ground next to me. I swiftly move to my feet, spreading them slightly apart and getting into my defensive stance. The crowd cheers in the background, but the noise becomes static in my ears.

I focus back on the tigress before me. She may have been quick and agile, but so am I. She has a weakness. I know it. I just have to find it. I watch her again and feel her tiger come forward, trying to assert dominance. I smile as I feel Kylah smile.

"Shall I show her who's more dominant?" she purrs beneath the surface.

"No. She's just trying to intimidate us. It's not going to work." She swings out with a right then left, but I block both. She comes back at me. We lock up again. This time I'm ready for the weight shift and counter her, flipping her the opposite way, so that I land on top of her.

What I wasn't ready for was the sharp slice of a blade across my side. It was effective in getting me off of her. I glanced down to my side, covering the slash with my hand. I remove it to see the line of blood streaked across my hand.

"Can we stop playing around and hurt her now?" The anger in Kylah's voice has my anger rising. Her emotions feeding my own.

"What do you think I've been trying to do? Why don't you help

me find her weakness?" I watch the woman across from me smirk as she stands once more.

"Considering she's favored her right both times she's attempted to take you down... how about you counter her weight and pin her again, but watch for the blade."

"Thanks Captain Obvious." I feel her smirk as the woman launches at me again. I counter once more and see the glint of the blade sticking out from the end of her long sleeve shirt. As she swings her arm towards me, I twist, grabbing her arm with the knife and pinning it to the ground.

"Not again," I grit out, holding her down. "Submit," I growl out, allowing Kylah to rise to the surface.

"Fine," she snarls between clenched teeth. "I submit."

I stand up and offer her a hand, but she smacks it away. I guess this isn't going to be friendly at all. Once more the sound of the crowd cheering sounds around me. Looking up, we were the last to finish.

"That was an exciting showing from the first trial," Calyope announces and the crowd continues to cheer. "We will have a ten-minute intermission before the second trial begins."

I slowly make my way over to the side where a medic is ready and waiting. He examines my side. Putting a bit of salve over it, he bandages it up and reassures me that I'm good to go for the next trial.

Calyope stands at the platform on the right side of the trial grounds.

"The next trial is about to begin. For the second trial we want to test our contestant's endurance and stamina. On my mark, the remaining eight contestants will run from the training grounds, through the path outlined in the woods behind us, around the castle and finally back here. In total it is a fifteen-mile run. If they don't make it before the timer is up, they will be disqualified. Contestants take your marks," she announces.

We line up at the starting line. Though the cut on my side is throbbing, I know I can do this. I've trained hard. I just need to put distance between myself and the other women. I can't get caught up in any plans to take me down.

"And go," Queen Calyope says, firing an air horn.

I take off at a sprint, trying to gain an early lead. I watch the markers as the trail weaves in and out of thick brush under the trees. I glance behind me and see that several of the women are on my heels. I push harder wanting to stay ahead of the pack.

Up ahead is a large drop off, with a stream five feet below. I try to time my steps and jump as my foot hits the edge. I soar over the gap and land hard on my injured side. What feels like a hot poker stabbing fires up. I wince and grit my teeth as I hobble to my feet and take off again.

A tiger passes me and winks as she shoots off. I need to focus and keep moving. I concentrate on the rhythm of my feet hitting the hard ground and soon I'm running faster again.

As I exit the tree line, I catch up with the tiger and we round the corner with the castle in site.

"You're not my direct competition so pass me if you like," she chuckles.

"Thanks," I grin and pull ahead.

She's right. The other women aren't going to worry about me because I'm the only panther here. They'll be focused on their direct competitors instead. My chest is burning, and my side has tears brimming my eyes, but I push through.

Finally, the trial grounds come into site. Just a little further, I remind myself. I push what little energy I have into one last sprint and cross the finish line. The crowd roars to life, cheering. I slow down and walk on the side to cool down and watch as the other competitors cross behind me.

In all, seven of the eight competitors cross before the time runs out. Queen Calyope sends a guard out to check on the missing woman.

"What a job well done," she announces when returning to the podium. "There will now be a fifteen-minute intermission before moving on to trial three."

I sit down on the provided bench while the medic checks my bandage then replaces. I guzzle down a bottle of water and my breathing returns to normal, though I'm half exhausted already.

CHAPTER THIRTEEN

Calyope stands from her box area and makes her way to the platform on the right side of trial grounds.

"It's time for the next trial," she announces to the crowd. "The third trial is an obstacle course. We want to see how the remaining seven contestants work out challenges in their cat form." The crowd cheers as Calyope pauses for a moment. "The order for this trial has been chosen at random. Ladies, please line up as I call your name."

We begin to line up and I find myself number four in the mix. The course is remarkably similar to the ones we practiced on, giving me confidence. I can do this. I've worked hard; hopefully, I don't make a mistake.

I watch carefully as the women run before me. Paying special attention to see what works and what trips them up. When it's my turn to go, I approach the first obstacle. It's a tall pole with a platform on top. Just like we practiced back at Nightfall.

I quickly make it to the top without any issues. I look across the course to the thin pipe that I must cross next. The slick metal glints beneath the light. I step one paw out onto the pipe. The coolness of the metal against my paw is a bit of a shock to the heat inside of me after having gone through the first trial. I take my time, getting all four paws on the pipe. My heart is beating heavy in my chest, but Kylah's in control and I have no choice but to sit back and watch as she works her way along the pipe.

Tall, metal spikes shoot up from the ground below, spooking Kylah and causing her to lose her balance. Her back paws slip from the pipe. Her claws extend and force themselves into the metal. The loud screech echoes across the arena. The tip of one of the spikes scraps across our rear right leg, and Kylah releases a growl. The crowd has gone completely silent as if holding their breath in anticipation of what's going to happen next.

"Just breathe," I speak calmly. *"We can do this."*

"I know," she grunts as she carefully shifts her weight and swings her rear haunches back up and onto the pipe. There's a collective sigh that's released from the crowd as we quickly make our way over the pipe to the next platform.

We both take our own sigh of relief to have finished that part of the obstacle course, but our relief is short lived as we examine the next obstacle in front of us.

The small forest in front of us looks like any other, but things aren't always as they appear. Kylah leaps from the platform to the first tree and we quickly find that throughout the trees are small, thin trip wires.

"What do you think happens if we hit one of those?" I ask, trying to hide the fear from my voice.

"I don't know, and I surely don't want to find out," she responds. Carefully we maneuver through the trees, making sure to avoid the small trip wires. As she leaps from one branch to the next, a small limb breaks off falling toward the small tripwire below us.

"Move!" I yell. Swiftly she moves across the branch,

jumping to the next as the limb breaks through the tripwire below us. Three arrows are released and fly by us, just as we clear the branch to the one next to it.

"Jesus, are they trying to kill us?" Kylah remarks as we stare behind us.

"I don't know, but I suggest we avoid any more of those trip wires. I don't want to find out what else those wires have in store for us," I remark.

"I agree." We continue to through the trees without any further incident. As we come to the other side of the small forest there's a pool of water below us.

I don't see anything that is outwardly dangerous about it, except a lot of cats have an aversion to water.

"Do you see anything I'm missing?" I ask Kylah.

"It's just water," she says.

"Then I guess we just swim," I reply.

I jump in and swim to the other side where AJ is waiting with a towel.

"You can shift back now. It's over," he smiles.

I shift back, take the towel, and dry off before putting the robe on. I wait here with the others while the last ones complete the course.

Once everyone has attempted the course, we are given another ten-minute intermission before the final trial... dominance. All seven of us are still in the running. Two lions, two tigers, two leopards, and me.

I make my way over from the third trial to the side line once more. Pulling the robe closer to my body, I feel the pangs of exhaustion begin to seep in. The mental and physical toll was more than I thought it would be.

"We only have one more trial. We can do this," Kylah echoes my words back to me. I smile. Our relationship may have started off a bit rocky but I'm not sure what I'd be without her.

"I know," I reply, smiling. She was right; we could do this. Everything was set for us to be the one true Queen. Once more Queen Calyope makes her way over to the platform in front of her box.

"The final trial is about to begin," she announces to the crowd, but instead of making her way back to her box, she joins the rest of us on the trial ground. She lifts the microphone, waiting for the crowd to calm before speaking.

"What an amazing bunch of competitors we have this time," Queen Calyope says. "Now for the trial you've all been waiting for, the dominance test. Each group of cats will be tested against each other. When the time comes for the panther, if she can kneel any of the strongest of us, she will take her throne."

She calls the leopards up first. They both attempt to dominate Queen Calyope and fail. It looks like she will keep her throne until the next trails.

The lions are called forward next. The audience waits in silence as the two women face each other and unleash their cats. Half of the audience drops to their knees while the women have a silent battle of wills. The taller blonde woman winces as the shorter brunette steadies her glare.

I wait in anticipation until the blonde takes a knee, glowering at her defeater.

"Congratulation's Zahara Huntsman," Queen Calyope says and the crowd roars to life.

Zahara steps forward and stands next to leopard queen to watch the final two challenges.

The tigers step forward, both petite redheads. The women square off but the one on the right is clearly more dominant as her competitor kneels almost immediately.

"Grisle Huntsman is the winner," Queen Calyope announces, the crowd nearly drowning her out. "Last but not least, time for our panther."

My stomach is churning as I step forward and allow Kylah to rise to the surface.

"Give it everything you've got," I encourage her.

"This should be fun," she purrs.

We let the dominance pour out of us and everyone takes a knee, including Queen Calyope. I look around and all the competitors are on their knees gritting their teeth, including the women that won their cats' crowns. What does this mean?

"Pull it back in, Lia," Queen Calyope instructs.

"Kylah, we need to stop," I say.

"You're no fun," she flicks her tail.

"It looks like Amelia Huntsman is our one and only queen from this point forward," Queen Calyope announces. "Long live the queen."

"Long live the queen!" The crowd echoes back then beings cheering.

"Wait, what about the other branches?" I ask in a quiet voice. "How will the trials work in the future now?"

Queen Calyope turns off the microphone. "You bowed everyone. There isn't anyone to rule by your side, kiddo. You won the entire thing, just as the prophecy foretold. I don't think there will be more trials, but we will cross that bridge when we get there," she explains. "I'll always be around to help, if you'll have me."

"Thank you," I reply, wrapping my arms around her.

CHAPTER FOURTEEN

The guys and Nathaniel rush down to the field and join me. I'm wrapped into a group hug as Nathaniel clears his throat.

"I told you so," he winks.

"Yes you did, but this is too much. There has always been four queens, but now it's just going to be me," I reply, trying to keep the nerves out of my voice. "I know the prophecy said it would happen, but it's just... I can't believe it really happened."

"You'll be a great queen. You care enough to listen and are surrounded by the right people; it won't be hard to adjust," he says.

"Sorry to break this up, but you need to go shower and change for your coronation. As soon as you're ready, it's happening," Queen Calyope says.

"AJ warned me it was fast, but it's almost overwhelming. Can I have a few minutes?" I ask, my eyes opening wide.

"Sorry, but it's always been our way. I had your dress delivered to your room so hurry up and get ready. A stylist will be waiting," she explains.

"On it," I reply.

The guys follow me as I make my way into the castle then leave me as I enter my room. I hop in the shower and clean up then slip into the elegant black, flowing dress that was laid out for me. The shoulders are surrounded by large plumage of feathers. I feel like it's wearing me instead of the other way around. As soon as I'm dressed, I hear a knock at the door.

The stylist introduces herself as Sophia. She sits me down and immediately gets to work, shaping my hair into an elaborate updo that hides my side shave then applies my makeup flawlessly.

I thank her then stand in front of the mirror. I barely recognize myself. Not too long ago I was a fifteen-year-old bear shifter, excited to join my clan on their first run. Funny how life never turns out how you expect it. Learning who I really am, coming to the Huntsman Clan was both the best and worst things that have ever happened to me.

I've found a new family, and friends that mean the world to me. Even though I lost someone so dear to me, I wouldn't change a thing. I take once last look around my room before stepping into the hallway where Demetria, Nathaniel, and my mates are waiting. Everything changes from this moment forward.

"You're going to come as yourself?" I ask, shocked to see my mother standing there.

"I've passed my job as head of security over to Nathaniel, so there's no point in pretending to be AJ any longer," she explains.

I nod in response.

"You ready for this?" Kenton asks.

"Do I have a choice?" I quip.

"No, but I still had to ask," he runs his hand through his hair.

"It will be ok. One thing at a time, right?" I reply.

We make our way into the throne room, which I haven't seen yet. My insides are churning, and everything is telling me to run the other way. I don't want this responsibility, but it's my life; it's my destiny.

We approach the large, gold gilded doors, and Demetria stops me.

"Only your mates can walk you the rest of the way. We are so proud of you," she says.

As the doors open, my mates surround me and we begin walking up the bright purple runner, leading to the thrones. The room is packed with the entire clan coming to see the new queen be crowned.

I wave and smile as we slowly proceed forward to where Queen Calyope is standing in front of the thrones. She directs me to stand in front of the ebony throne then silences the room.

A man with a crown and scepter on purple pillows joins her. First, she takes the crown.

"Amelia Huntsman, do you agree to serve the shifter community and rule in a just and fair way?" she asks.

"I do," I reply, my voice ringing clear throughout the quiet room.

She motions for me to sit so I do as she instructs.

"Heavy is the crown to remind you of the responsibility to your people," she announces as she places the crown on my head.

"This scepter represents your rule, may it be long and fruitful." She takes the scepter from the awaiting pillow and places it in my hand.

"I present to you Queen Amelia," she says then removes her crown and places it on the pillow she took mine from.

The crowd erupts in cheers, which are nearly deafening in this quiet room.

My mates join me, circling my throne as we take it all in. It all happened. I'm the queen and this is my kingdom. For once, all is right in the world.

My husbands and I sit in the living room watching our toddler play at our feet with the wrapped presents under the tree.

A knock at the door has Reid jumping to his feet to answer it.

Rachael, Jack, and their two kids come in, followed by Calyope and her three husbands.

"Merry Christmas," Jack says, scooping up my son in his arms giving him a squeeze.

"Merry Christmas," I smile at him.

Demetria and Nathaniel show up a short time later hand in hand. We settle in and chat until another knock at the door. Spence opens it and my adoptive parents, brother and his wife and two children come in.

I can't believe how much has changed in the last few years. We finished school while Calyope was my acting queen. I focused on learning everything I needed to so I could rule fairly, with Calyope being my right hand and most trusted advisor.

Our wedding was so well received that shifters from all

over the world come to witness it. I had both of my dads give me away. My family has grown so much, and our house is filled with love.

I can't wait to share the news I got this morning with everyone.

"Now that we are all here together for Christmas, we have something to tell you," I grin. "We are pregnant again!"

After rounds of hugs and congratulations, we open our presents and enjoy lunch together before dinner with the community. I'm so grateful for how my life has turned out in the end.

ABOUT THE AUTHOR

Rose Alexander

Rose lives in the Midwest with her husband, kids and three cats. She enjoys crafting in her free time and watching movies with her family.
Rose Alexander Author Page
Rose's Reverie - Readers Group
Rose Alexander - Instagram
Rose Alexander Twitter
Rose Alexander Pinterest
Academy of Broken Dreams Reader's Group (Co-writes)